"I just lost my job."

The words burned in Maggie's throat.

"I'm sorry. I—" Kevin reached out to her but she stepped back.

"You basically accused the chairman of the board of the museum of stealing a priceless artifact." She shook with anger.

"I could have been more diplomatic. I wasn't thinking."

"That's just it. You never think about me. When we were together in college, it was all about you."

"It was never about me. It was about making money so my mom didn't have to struggle anymore."

"That doesn't explain why you dumped me. We were planning a life together after graduation. A family. And then just like that, you were gone. And now you want a second chance?"

"Walking away from you was the biggest mistake of my life. I've always regretted it and I'm more sorry than I can ever express. I know I hurt you—"

"You have no idea," she hissed, the truth waiting for her to speak it aloud.

UNDER LOCK AND KEY

K.D. RICHARDS

Harlequin
INTRIGUE

Harlequin®
INTRIGUE™

Recycling programs
for this product may
not exist in your area.

ISBN-13: 978-1-335-45698-4

Under Lock and Key

Copyright © 2024 by Kia Dennis

Harlequin Enterprises ULC
22 Adelaide St. West, 41st Floor
Toronto, Ontario M5H 4E3, Canada
www.Harlequin.com

Printed in Lithuania

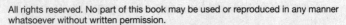

MIX
Paper | Supporting
responsible forestry
FSC® C021394

K.D. Richards is a native of the Washington, DC, area, who now lives outside Toronto with her husband and two sons. You can find her at kdrichardsbooks.com.

Books by K.D. Richards

Harlequin Intrigue

West Investigations

Visit the Author Profile page at Harlequin.com.

CAST OF CHARACTERS

Kevin Lombard—West Security and Investigations private investigator.

Maggie Scott—Curator at the Larimer Museum and suspect in the theft of the Viperé ruby.

Tess Stenning—Head of West Security and Investigations' West Coast office.

Detective Gill Francois—LAPD detective investigating the theft.

Robert Gustev—Maggie's boss.

Carter Tutwilder—Chairman of the board of the Larimer Museum.

Chapter One

Maggie Scott looked around the dimly lit museum gallery, exhausted but content. She'd done it. The donors' open house for the Viperé ruby exhibit had been a rousing success. The classical music that had played softly in the background during the night was silent now, but the air of sophistication and sense of reverence still filled the room. Soft spotlights lit the priceless paintings on the wall while a brighter beam shone down on what was literally the crown jewel of the exhibit. The Viperé ruby glowed under the light like a blood red sun.

Maggie stood in front of the glass case with the almost empty bottle of champagne she'd procured from the caterers before they'd left and a flute. She poured what little was left in the bottle into the flute and toasted herself.

"Congratulations to me." She downed half the liquid in the glass. Her eyes passed over the gallery space with a mixture of awe, satisfaction and pride. The night had been the culmination of a year's worth of labor. A decade of work if she counted undergraduate and graduate school and the handful of jobs she'd held at other museums before joining the Larimer Museum as an assistant curator three years earlier. It had taken a massive amount of work to ensure the success of the display and the open house for the donors and board members, who got a first look at the highly anticipated exhibit. As one of two assistant curators up for a possible promotion to curator and with the director of the British museum who'd loaned the Viperé ruby to the relatively small Larimer Museum watching her, she was under a great deal of pressure from a great many people. But the night had been an unmitigated success, so said her boss, and she was hopeful that she was now a shoo-in for the promotion.

Maggie stepped closer to the jewel, reaching out with her free hand and almost grazing the glass. The spotlight hit the ruby, creating a rainbow of glittering light around her. She raised the champagne flute to her lips and spoke, "To the Viperé ruby and all the other pieces of art that have inspired, challenged and united humanity in ways words cannot express."

She finished the champagne and stood for a moment, taking in the energy and vitality that emanated from the works around her.

Maggie was abruptly yanked from her reverie by the sound of a soft thud. She and Carl Downy were the only two people who were still in the building. Carl was the retired cop who provided security at night for the museum. Mostly, that meant he walked the three floors of the renovated and repurposed Victorian building that was itself a work of art between naps during his nine-hour shift.

A surge of unease traveled through her. She gripped the empty champagne bottle tightly and called out, "Carl, is that you?"

A moment passed without a response.

Unease was replaced with concern. Carl was getting on in years. He could have fallen or had a medical emergency of some type.

Maggie stepped into the even more dimly lit hallway connecting the rooms, the galleries as her boss liked to call them, on the main floor. The thud had sounded as if it had come from the front of the museum, but all she saw was pitch black in that direction. She knew the nooks and crannies of the museum as well as she knew her own house. Normally, she loved wandering through the space, leisurely taking in the pieces. Even though she'd seen each of them dozens of times, she always found herself noticing something new, some aspect or feature of the pieces she'd overlooked. That was one of the reasons she loved art. It was always teaching, always changing, even when it stayed the same.

But she didn't love it at the moment. The museum was eerily still and quiet.

Suddenly, a dark-clad figure stepped out of the shadows. He wore a mask, but she could tell he was a male. That was all she had time to process before the figure charged at her.

Her heartbeat thundered, and a voice in her head told her to run, but her feet felt melted to the floor. The bottle and champagne flute slid from her hands, shattering against the polished wood planks.

The intruder slammed her back into the wall, knocking the breath out of her. Before she had time to recover, he backhanded her across the face with a beefy gloved hand.

Pain exploded on the side of her face.

She slid along the wall, instinct forcing her to try to get away even as her conscious brain still struggled to process what was happening. But her assailant grabbed her arm, stopping her escape.

Her vision was blurred by the blow to her face, and the mask the intruder wore covered all but his dark brown eyes. Still, she was aware of her assailant raising his hand a second time, his fist clenched.

Her limbs felt like they were stuck in molasses, but she tried to raise her arm to deflect the blow.

Too slowly, as it turned out.

The intruder hit her on the side of her head, the impact causing excruciating pain before darkness descended and her world faded to black.

KEVIN LOMBARD'S PHONE RANG, dragging him out of a dreamless sleep at just after one in the morning.

"Lombard."

"Kevin, hey, sorry to wake you." The voice of his new boss, Tess Stenning, flowed over the phone line. "We have a problem. An assault and theft at the Larimer Museum, one of our newer clients. Since you are West Investigation's new director of corporate and institutional accounts, that makes it your problem."

Kevin groaned. He'd only been on the job for three weeks, but Tess was right, his division, his problem. It didn't matter that he hadn't overseen the installation of the security system at the Larimer. He'd looked over the file, as he'd done with all of the security plans that West Security and Investigations' new West Coast office had installed in the six months since they'd been open, so he had an idea of what the gallery security looked like.

West Security and Investigations was one of the premier security and private investigation firms on the East Coast. Run primarily by brothers Ryan and Shawn West, with a little help from their two older brothers, James and Brandon, West Security and Investigations had recently opened a West Coast office in Los Angeles, headed up by Tess Stenning, a long-time West operative and damn good private investigator. If he'd been asked a year ago whether he would ever consider joining a private investigations firm, even one with as sterling a reputation as West Security and Investigations, he'd have laughed.

But staying in Idyllwild had become untenable. A friend of a friend had recommended he reach out to Tess, and after a series of interviews with her and Ryan West, he'd been offered the job. Moving to Los Angeles had been an adjustment, but he was settling in.

He searched his memory for the details of the museum's security. Despite West Security and Investigations' recommendation that the museum update its entire security system, the gallery's board of directors had only approved the security specifications for the Viperé ruby. Shortsighted, he'd noted when he'd read the file, and now he had the feeling that he was about to be proven right.

Tess gave him the sparse details that she'd gotten from her contact on the police force. Someone had broken into the museum, attacked a curator and a guard and made off with the ruby. He ended the call and dragged himself into the bathroom for a quick shower. Ten years on the police force had conditioned him to getting late night— or early morning, as it were—phone calls. The shower helped wake him, and he set his coffee machine to brew while he quickly dressed then pulled up the museum's file on his West-issued tablet. A little more than thirty minutes after he'd gotten the call from Tess, he was headed out.

He arrived at the Larimer Museum twenty minutes later, thankful that most of Los Angeles was still asleep or out partying and not on the roads. He showed his ID to the police officer manning the door and was waved in. Officers milled about in the lobby, but he caught sight of Tess down a short hall toward the back of the Victorian building, talking to a small man in a rumpled suit and haphazardly knotted blue tie. The man waved his hands in obvious distress while it looked like Tess tried to console him.

Kevin made his way toward the pair. In the room twenty feet from where they stood, a police technician worked gathering evidence from the break-in.

"This is going to ruin us. The Larimer Museum will be ruined, and I'll never get another job as curator again." The man wiped the back of his hand over his brow.

Tess gave Kevin a nod. "Mr. Gustev, this is my colleague Kevin Lombard. Kevin, Robert Gustev, managing director and head curator of the Larimer Museum."

Gustev ignored Kevin's outstretched hand. He pointed his index figure at Tess. "This is your fault."

"West Investigations is going to do its best to identify the perpetrators and retrieve the ruby."

Gustev swiped his hand over his brow again. "I can't believe this is happening."

The man looked on the verge of being sick.

"Mr. Gustev—" Tess started.

"You were supposed to protect the ruby."

"If you recall, we did make several recommendations for upgrading the museum's security, which you and the Larimer's board of directors rejected," Tess said pointedly.

Gustev's face reddened, his jowls shaking in anger.

"Mr. Gustev," Kevin said before the curator had a chance to respond to Tess. "We are going to do everything we can to recover the ruby. It would help if you took Tess and I through everything that happened up until the time the intruder assaulted you."

"Me? No, it wasn't me that the thief attacked."

Kevin frowned. On the phone, Tess had said the guard and the curator had been attacked.

"It was my assistant curator who confronted the thief." Gustev frowned. "She's speaking with the police detective in her office right now."

"Oh, well, why don't you tell us what you know, and we'll speak to her once the police have finished."

Gustev ran them through a detailed description of the party that had taken place earlier that night. Kevin pressed the man on whether anything out of the ordinary happened at the party or in the days before, but Gustev swore that nothing of note had occurred.

The curator waved a hand at Tess. "I have to call the board members." He turned and hurried off down the hall, ascending a rear staircase.

Tess's eyes stayed trained on the retreating man's back until he disappeared on the second-floor landing. She let out a labored sigh. "This is going to turn into a you-know-what show if we don't get a handle on it fast."

Kevin's stomach turned over because she was right. "I'm not sure we can avoid that, but I'll do my best to get to the bottom of things as quickly as possible." He turned to look at the activity taking place in the room to the right of where they stood.

Glass sparkled on top of a podium covered with a black velvet blanket. A numbered yellow cone marked the shards as evidence. A crime scene tech made her way around the room, systematically photographing and bagging anything of note.

Tess groaned. "Someone managed to break into the building and steal the Viperé ruby, a ruby the size of your fist and worth more than the gross domestic product of my hometown of Missoula."

His eyebrow quirked up. "Sounds like a lot."

"Try two hundred fifty million a lot."

Kevin gave a low whistle. "That's a lot."

Tess cut him a look. "A lot of problems for us. I'm afraid Gustev—" she nodded toward the staircase that the curator had ascended moments earlier "—is going to throw himself out of a window."

The curator was more than a little bit on edge, but who could blame him. "The thief attacked the assistant curator but left her alive?"

Tess nodded. "The night guard and one of the assistant curators were knocked unconscious by the thief, apparently."

Kevin frowned. "What was an assistant curator still doing here so late?"

"That I don't know." Tess shrugged. "But the museum had a party tonight to kick off the opening of the Viperé ruby exhibit. The board, donors and other muckety mucks, drinking, dancing and, undoubtedly, opening their wallets."

"Undoubtedly," he said, turning his attention back to the crime scene technician at work.

Tess shook her head. "The guard was out cold when the EMTs arrived. They took him to the hospital. He's on the older side, former cop, though, so he's tough. The curator is in her office. Declined transportation to the hospital."

"Sounds like she's pretty tough, too."

Tess shrugged. "Or stupid. Detective Gill Francois is questioning her now."

He frowned. He hadn't had the pleasure of working with Francois yet, but he'd heard of him. The detective was a bulldog.

Tess chuckled. "Don't do that. Gill's good people. I've

already talked to him. He's agreed to let us tag along on the case, as long as we play nice and keep him in the loop regarding anything we find out."

He felt one of his eyebrows arch up. "And he'll do the same?"

Tess rolled her eyes. "You know how it goes. He says he will but…"

"Yeah, *but.*" He did know how it went. He'd been one of the boys in blue not so long ago.

"Listen, I made sure West Investigations covered its rear regarding our advice to the board of directors of the museum to upgrade the entire system." Tess waved a hand in the air. "I told them that the security they'd authorized for the Viperé ruby left them open to possible theft, but they didn't want to spend the money and figured the locked and alarmed case along with the on-site twenty-four-hour security guard was enough."

"Didn't want to pony up the money?"

Tess tapped her nose then sighed. "Still, this is going to be a black mark on West Investigations if we don't figure out what happened here quickly. I know you've barely gotten settled in, but do you think you're up for the job?"

"Absolutely," he answered without reservation. "The first thing I want to do is get the security recordings and the alarm logs and get the exact time when the case was broken. We'll also need to figure out what the thief used to break the glass." He pulled the same type of small notebook he'd used when he was a police detective out of his jacket along with the small pen he kept hooked in the spiral. His tablet was in the computer case that hung from his shoulder, but he preferred the old-fashioned methods. Writing out his notes and thoughts helped him remember things better and think things through. "Of course, shatterproof glass isn't invincible, but it would have taken a great deal of force and a strong weapon to do it." He scratched out notes on his thoughts before they got away from him.

Tess cleared her throat. "The alarm went off just after eleven, triggered by the curator after she'd regained consciousness. Getting more specific than that is going to be a problem, at least with regards to the alarm logs."

Kevin looked up from his notebook. "Why?"

Tess looked more than a little green around the gills.

His stomach turned over, anticipating that whatever she was about to say wasn't going to be good.

"Because the alarm didn't go off," she said.

"The alarm didn't go off." Kevin repeated the words back to Tess as if they didn't make any sense to him. Then again, they didn't. "How is that possible?"

"That is a very good question."

He and Tess turned toward the sound of the voice.

A man Kevin would have made as a cop no matter where they'd met descended the back staircase.

Kevin's gaze moved to the woman coming down the stairs next to him, and his world stopped.

The man and woman halted in front of him and Tess.

"Hello, Kevin." The words floated from Maggie's lips on a wisp of a breath.

"Hello, Maggie."

Maggie Scott. His college girlfriend and, at one point, the woman he'd imagined spending his life with.

Chapter Two

Kevin's eyes swept over Maggie, drinking her in. Her dark hair was mussed and fell in tangled ringlets around the soft curve of her cocoa-colored cheeks. When he'd thought of her over the years, it had always been as he'd remembered her. A co-ed in jeans that hugged her voluptuous curves and CalSci T-shirts that he'd loved peeling off her. But now she was dressed in a black sheath cocktail dress and heels that accentuated long, smooth legs that had him remembering the ecstasy he'd felt having them wrapped around his waist.

"You know each other?" Detective Francois's voice pulled him back to the present. The detective's gaze darted between Kevin and Maggie.

"Yeah," Kevin answered.

At the same time, Maggie said, "We were acquaintances in college."

Acquaintances. They'd been much more than acquaintances. For a while, he thought they would spend the rest of their lives together. But then the NFL had come knocking, and he'd let hubris and arrogance turn him into a fool. He'd wanted to start his new life unencumbered, so he'd broken things off with Maggie.

It was, to date, the biggest mistake he'd ever made in his life.

Pale skin shone under the thinning wisps of hair on the top of Francois's head. Kevin put him somewhere in his early fifties, but the intelligence that sparked in the man's eyes said it wouldn't be easy to get anything over on him. It was clear he suspected there was more than a mere college friendship between Kevin and Maggie, but the detective didn't push. At least, not yet.

"What is this about the alarm not going off?" Francois looked at Maggie with suspicion in his gaze. "I thought you said you triggered the alarm when you regained consciousness?"

"I did," Maggie said, defensiveness in her tone. She wrapped her arms around her torso.

"She did," Tess interjected, "but the alarm should have gone off automatically when the intruder entered the building and when the case with the Viperé ruby was opened, but it didn't."

"And why didn't it?" Francois demanded.

Tess rubbed her temples. "We are looking into it, but it appears that someone turned the system off just before the theft occurred."

"Turned it off?" Detective Francois said. "Can someone just hit a switch and shut the thing down?"

"It's not that easy," Kevin said, his eyes straying to Maggie again. The shock he'd seen in her eyes when they'd first landed on him was gone, replaced by a guarded coolness. She had the beginnings of a shiner growing around her left eye. A bandage was affixed to her right temple.

He fought the urge to hurt the person who'd put their hands on her.

"We can discuss this further in a moment. I was just going to have an officer take Ms. Scott home." Francois nodded at a uniformed officer, who hurried over.

"If it's okay with you, Detective, I'd like to ask Ms. Scott a few questions," Kevin said.

Francois made a face. "I'm sure Ms. Scott is exhausted. Maybe it can wait until tomorrow?"

"It's okay," Maggie said. "I'll do whatever I can to help. I can't believe someone stole the Viperé ruby."

"Let's start there. I'm sure you've told Detective Francois already, and Tess of course knows about the ruby from having set up the security, but would you mind telling me about the gem?"

"The Viperé ruby from the Isle Bení," Maggie started, appearing to perk up just a bit. "It's a rare, priceless jewel with a rich, contested history."

"Contested." Kevin looked up from the notes he'd been taking.

"Isle Bení is a small island off the coast of Greece. How exactly the jewel got into the hands of the British government is hotly debated to this day, but somewhere around the turn of the nineteenth century, the ruby went missing only to be 'found'—" Maggie made air quotes "—in the private collection of a British millionaire. I'm going to jump over a ton of history here. Let's just say the ruby changed hands multiple times, ultimately ending up property of the British government but the subject of multiple lawsuits arguing that it was stolen from the Bení people and is rightfully theirs. A number of lawsuits have been pending for years."

"Got it," Kevin said, making notes. The story didn't sound all that unusual. He knew that a lot of cultural artifacts had contested ownership.

"Beyond the pricelessness of the piece, the ruby is also the subject of a legend," Maggie continued.

A legend. Well, that was interesting.

"Many of the citizens of the island believe that the jewel was the reason their land was prosperous and safe for many centuries before the British discovered it. Since the ruby was discovered in British hands, the island has contended with many of the issues other small islands have had to contend with. A struggling economy. Youth fleeing for greener pastures. Globalization."

"It doesn't seem fair to blame that on a ruby," Detective Francois said. "As you said, many places are dealing with the same issues."

Maggie shrugged. "Fair or not, that's what the legend holds."

"This is great background. Let's jump ahead a few hundred years or so to what happened here tonight," Kevin said with an encouraging smile.

Maggie let out a long, deep breath.

Kevin watched as the tension that had left her shoulders when she'd been talking about the ruby returned.

She crossed her arms over her torso. "I don't know where to start."

"Just start at the beginning," he said soothingly. "I understand you had some kind of party here at the museum tonight."

Maggie nodded. "Yes, a donors' open house. We have them before every big opening. We invite the big donors and those we hope will become big donors, the board, politicians, reporters and anyone else we can think of that could help us with funding and getting the word out about the museum and the work we do."

"How many people would you say were in attendance tonight?"

"Um…a hundred fifty. Maybe a little more. We are constrained by space limitations."

"Okay." Kevin nodded encouragingly. "When did the donors' open house end?"

"The last board member and Mr. Gustev left around nine thirty. The caterers were here for another forty-five minutes."

"But you stayed later? Why?"

A faint smile ticked her lips upward. "I wanted a moment to celebrate my success. The exhibit was my baby. Robert and the board had the ultimate sign-off on the loan of the Viperé ruby from the London Natural History Museum, but I was the one who broached the exchange and shepherded it through the thorny maze of contracts, permits and diplomacy that these kinds of trades require."

Kevin nodded. "That makes sense. So you were here in this room?" He jerked his chin in the direction of the shattered glass around the display case.

"Gallery, we call each of the rooms *galleries*. And yes, I was in the gallery that hosted the exhibit when I heard a thud. I stepped out into the hall to investigate, and a man in black just appeared out of the shadows." A small tremble went through her.

He had a sudden urge to wrap her in his arms.

"It all happened so fast. I know that's a cliché, but it really did happen so fast. The guy hit me, twice I think, maybe three times. I know I lost consciousness but not for too long." Her face scrunched. "At least, I don't think it was too long. The next thing I remember was waking up on the floor here in the hall. It took me a minute to stand without my head spinning, then I made my way to the security office where Carl usually sits. He was on the floor, blood around his head. I grabbed the office phone and called 911."

Kevin scribbled out everything she'd said in his note-pad. "Can you describe the man?"

She shook her head, then stopped, wincing. "He was dressed in all black and had a mask over his face. I'm sorry that's all I can tell you."

"But you're sure it was a man?"

"Yes."

That was something, but not much.

"Did you, or maybe Carl, turn off the alarm after every-one left?" Tess said. "Maybe so you could take the jewel out of the case?"

Maggie's forehead furrowed. "Absolutely not. I mean I can't speak for Carl, but I don't know why he would. And I can say for a fact that I didn't turn it off. Why?"

"It looks like someone did," Detective Francois said.

Maggie's big hazel eyes widened even further. "Some-one shut off the alarm?"

"Using an administrative code on site," Tess said. "I'd have to talk to Mr. Gustev to find out exactly who the code belonged to."

Maggie's arms tightened around her midsection, and her face blanched. "There's only one code. Mr. Gustev, Kim and I, we all used the same code." Tess's expression darkened. "But I showed Mr. Gustev how to create unique codes for each employee he wanted to have access to the system. That way, we could track who turns it on and off. I showed him how to do it."

"And Kim and I told him that we should all have our own codes, but he didn't think that was necessary. Said it would mean changing codes every time someone left for a new job and that having more than one code meant there was more chances for a code to get into the wrong hands."

"But it's the exact opposite." Tess's voice rose. "One

code makes it all the more likely that someone could get their hands on it!"

Maggie's expression was apologetic, even though it didn't appear she had anything to be sorry about. "I know, but Mr. Gustev has never been very accepting of new technology. We only got the upgraded security system because it was a condition in the loan of the Viperé ruby."

"I'm sorry. Who is Kim?" Kevin interjected.

"Kim Sumika," Detective Francois answered his question.

"The other assistant curator here," Maggie added. "She helped me set up, but she had a terrible migraine come on and had to miss the opening gala."

Detective Francois asked, "Were you, Ms. Sumika and Mr. Gustev the only three with the code to turn off the alarm?"

"And Carl and the day guards." Maggie's chin jerked up. "Wait. You can't possibly think that someone who works here had anything to do with stealing the Viperé ruby?"

No one spoke.

Maggie shook her head vehemently. "That's not possible. None of us would do this. We're like a family here. We've all had thorough background checks, and we've all worked for the Larimer for years."

Kevin had seen too much to discount anything. It was often the people closest that had the greatest power to betray the most.

The expression on Tess's and Detective Francois's faces said they were thinking along the same lines.

"Okay, let's set the alarm aside for now," he said, taking charge of the questioning again. "Was the man carrying anything? A hammer or some sort of baton?"

Maggie shook her head slowly this time, whether it was because she was thinking or to keep from wincing a second time, he wasn't sure. "No, nothing that I could see, but I was startled and terrified. He could have had something with him. I know he hit me with his hand. His fist actually, it is one thing I can remember very clearly."

Kevin's anger flared again. He hoped he found out who this guy was before the cops did. He'd make sure to get a few shots. Any man who hit a woman didn't deserve to be called a man in his book.

Maggie raised a shaky hand to the bandage on her forehead.

"I think that's enough for tonight," Detective Francois said.

Kevin nodded his agreement and closed his notebook. "Maggie, why don't you let me give you a lift home?"

"Thanks, but I have my car."

"You've been through a lot tonight. Let Kevin drive you home," Tess interjected. "If you give me your car keys and address, I'll make sure your car is in your driveway before you wake up tomorrow morning."

Maggie hesitated.

"Really, Maggie. It would be my pleasure to see you home safely." He gave her what he hoped was a reassuring smile. Tess was right. She'd been hit over the head hard enough to black out, and he wanted to make sure she got home safely.

She hesitated for a second longer. "Well, if you're sure. Yes, thank you, I'd love to go home now."

He waited for her to fall into step next to him, staying on guard in case she needed a hand. Head wounds could be tricky, and the last thing he wanted was for her to get woozy and fall.

Chapter Three

Kevin drove them through the early morning traffic with ease. It was far too early for most commuters to be on the streets, thankfully.

Maggie sat in the passenger seat, her head resting against the side window. She'd answered with a soft "thank you" when Kevin held the passenger door open for her to get into the car but hadn't spoken otherwise. She could tell Kevin had more questions he wanted to ask her, but she was grateful when he didn't push.

It was a struggle to take in oxygen. She knew the Viperé ruby was gone, but she still struggled to process exactly what that meant. For her and for the Larimer.

Her throat constricted even further. Once word got out that the museum had let the priceless jewel be stolen, they'd never get another museum to agree to let them showcase their pieces. Not to mention the donors who would drop them, unwilling to be associated with a museum surrounded by scandal.

She would probably lose her job. Heck, the museum might close altogether.

Her head began to spin. She could feel a panic attack coming on. Great. That was just what she needed. To embarrass herself in front of the security specialist.

Breathe, breathe, she ordered herself. After several minutes, the spinning stopped, and she felt her pulse slowing to a normal speed.

She looked across the car to see if Kevin had noticed her near meltdown. His chiseled chin was still in profile, his dark brown eyes trained straight ahead at the windshield.

"Thank you for driving me home," she said, breaking the silence as they neared her street. "It's kind of you."

"I'm just doing my job."

Just doing his job. He was still painfully clear about where his priorities lay, and it wasn't with her.

"Of course. Your job."

His career was the reason he'd broken up with her in college. Or the career he'd planned on having as a wide receiver in the NFL. Unfortunately, a torn ACL during the preseason had ended his career before it really began. She was embarrassed to remember how she'd harbored a hope that he'd return and somehow they'd find their way back to each other. But he hadn't returned or reached out to her. He'd enlisted in the military. And she'd met and married Ellison, moved on with her life, but she'd never stopped thinking about him.

"I didn't mean it like that. I just meant West Security and Investigations was hired to provide security to the Larimer, and as far as I'm concerned that includes its employees. That's you. I'm sorry we failed you tonight."

They made the rest of the drive in a long awkward silence. Finally, he turned into the long driveway that led to her rental, a former carriage house situated behind Kim's much larger Tudor-style home. He stopped in front of the carriage home and put the car in Park.

He hit his seat belt release. "Let me help you into the house."

She unlatched her own seat belt and waited for Kevin to open the passenger door.

He offered his hand to help her out of the car. The skin-to-skin contact set off fireworks in her. Did he feel it too?

She gave herself a mental shake. It didn't matter. He couldn't have been clearer. Just doing his job. Heck, she'd seen his face when Detective Francois had implied she or someone from the Larimer might be involved in the theft. He wasn't attracted to her. He suspected she was involved in the Viperé's theft.

She pulled her hand back. "I think I've got it."

Kevin shut the car door, and they started for the cottage. "This is a nice place. How'd you find it?"

"Through my friend. Kimberly Sumika." She was moving slowly. Her entire body aching.

He frowned. "The other assistant curator?"

She nodded. "Yes. She owns the big house." She cocked her head toward the Tudor. "I rent the carriage house from her. She and I were friends in grad school, but lost touch after graduation. When Ellison died, she reached out."

Kevin shot a glance across the dark interior of the car. "Ellison. Your husband?"

"Ex-husband. We'd been divorced for a few months when he died. He'd…had some troubles at his job before his death. He had been charged with embezzling five hundred thousand dollars from his accounting firm." She shifted in the passenger seat. It was awkward telling Kevin about Ellison, but she'd rather he heard the story from her.

She cleared her throat and continued. "Even though Ellison was gone, the scandal that swirled around him wasn't. A lot of people in New York thought I was in on the theft or at least knew about it. It was horrible. I lost my job. No museum in New York would hire me. Kim got in touch and told me about an opening at the Larimer, where she worked. She put in a good word for me, and I got the job, so I moved back to California. She really went to bat for me to get the job."

"And she gave you a place to live. Sounds like a good friend." Kevin helped her up the two front steps.

She reached into the front pocket of her purse for her keys. "At a steep discount off market rates. She is a great friend." Worry niggled at her.

After dialing 911, she'd called both Robert and Kim, but Kim hadn't answered her phone. Maggie had left a message for her explaining the break-in. Kim loved the museum as much as she did. Why hadn't she at least returned the call?

She turned to look at the Tudor. The back door stood open.

She grasped his forearm. "Kevin. Something is wrong."

She felt his body tense beside her. He slipped in front of her, pinning her between the front door of the cottage and his large body.

"What is it?"

"Kim's back door is open." She pointed. "She'd never forget to lock her doors."

His body stiffened even more. "You go inside. I'll check it out."

He bounded off the porch stairs and moved like liquid across the lawn and up the Tudor's back porch staircase.

She was exhausted and injured, but there was no way she was going to cower in her house when Kim could need help. She followed Kevin across the backyard and into the Tudor.

The back door opened directly onto the kitchen. The Larimer didn't pay them anywhere near enough to afford a four-bedroom, three-bathroom detached home in the Los Angeles suburbs. Kim had inherited the house from her parents, and the mortgage-free home had allowed her the ability to use her salary to make extensive upgrades. The kitchen was modern, designed so that the appliances blended in with the cabinets.

The interior of the house was dark, and Kevin had disappeared somewhere inside.

Dread twisted in Maggie's stomach. She took a deep breath, attempting to calm her nerves, and made her way down the short hallway from the kitchen to the front of the house.

Kevin met her at the entrance to the living room. "You shouldn't go in there."

"Why? What's wrong? Where is Kim?"

Kevin tried to move her backward, but she skirted around him.

A sob caught in her throat.

Kevin wrapped his arm around her shoulders and turned her away from the living room. But not fast enough.

Kim was slumped on the sofa. She appeared to be asleep, but her skin was ashen and gray. Her eyes stared forward, empty, at nothing.

Kim wasn't asleep.

She was dead.

Chapter Four

Kevin took Maggie back to her cottage and got her settled before returning to the front porch of the Tudor to wait for the authorities. EMTs and officers responded quickly, as did Detective Francois. He pulled up right behind the ambulance although there was no need for anyone to hurry. Kim Sumika was beyond help.

The property around the house had been taped off with yellow crime scene tape, drawing neighbors out of their homes to gawk at the goings-on despite the early hour.

Francois paused on his way into the house only long enough to have Kevin recount how he and Maggie had found Kim's body and to ask him not to go anywhere. That had been thirty minutes ago, and Kevin was itching to go check on Maggie. He was just about to let the heavyset, young, uniformed officer with puffy eyes who manned the door know that he could be found in the cottage at the rear of the property when he heard Francois call out for him to come inside.

Kevin stepped into the house and found the detective standing in the entryway to the living room. The detective was alone in the room, the crime scene technicians having not yet arrived.

Francois turned his gray eyes on Kevin. "You're a former cop."

It wasn't a question, not really. He was sure the detective had checked him, Tess and West Investigations out. "San Jacinto PD. Seven years."

Francois nodded. "Tell me what you see."

Kevin looked at the scene. Kim's body sat on the sofa. She was in her late thirties or early forties and fit. It looked almost as if she'd been settling in for a relaxing night in front of the television. She wore loose-fitting pajama pants, a Clippers T-shirt and slippers that showed off electric blue toenails. An open bottle of wine and a mostly eaten bowl of popcorn sat on the coffee table. The television facing the sofa was off. An ordinary night except for the needle on the carpet at Kim's feet and the belt that was looped around the dead woman's right arm like a tourniquet. On the coffee table in front of the couch were various other indicators of drug use.

"Possible overdose."

Francois's bushy brows made a V over his nose. "Possible?"

Kevin shrugged. "I don't like making assumptions. It looks like an overdose based on the limited information in front of me. The television was off when I found her. You should check to see if it's one of those energy savers that turns itself off after a certain amount of time sitting idle."

Francois smiled slightly and made a note on his phone. "Would you like to take a closer look?" He waved for Kevin to come farther into the room.

He would. He stepped into the living room, careful to stay on the pathway that Francois had already marked off with police tape. The fact that Francois had made sure to delineate a confined pathway for the techs and any other required personnel marked him as a true professional. It was important to make sure that no one muddied the scene more than necessary.

Kevin scanned the room, turning slowly, marking the space on a mental grid and noting anything that seemed out of place or relevant. The first thing he noticed was that the carpet appeared to have been vacuumed recently. As in so recently that there were still lines in the material from the vacuum wheels.

He stepped closer to Kim's body. There were indications of track marks on both her arms, but they appeared to be old and scarred over. She had clearly been a drug user at some point in her life. Had she relapsed? It was possible. Relapse among former drug users was common even after years of sobriety. Many former users didn't realize that starting up with drugs again after years of being clean could have immediate and devastating effects on a body that had already been through so much.

Kevin turned back to Francois. "Can I take a look around the house?"

Francois nodded. "Certainly. We can look together."

They moved as carefully through the rest of the house as they had in the living room. There wasn't much to see. Four bedrooms and two bathrooms upstairs. A den, dining room, bathroom and kitchen on the main floor. The basement was unfinished, and it looked as if Kim used it as a gym and storage space.

No sign of anything amiss or disturbed anywhere except in the living room.

He and Francois stepped back into the foyer just as the crime scene technicians walked through the front door with their equipment.

"You should make sure they get photographs of everything in the living room, including shots of the carpet leading from the doorway to where Kim is sitting," Kevin said to Francois, hoping the detective didn't get piqued and decide he was overstepping.

Francois cocked his head to one side. "Why?"

"Look at it." Kevin, Francois and the crime scene tech turned toward the living room. "Doesn't it strike you as odd?"

"Odd?" Francois said.

"I see what you mean." The tech, a tall, easily six-foot-six, woman with vibrant green hair, nodded excitedly.

"Well, I don't." Francois frowned. "Can someone clue me in?"

"There are vacuum lines in the carpet but no footprint impressions," Kevin answered. "How could she have gotten to the sofa without mussing the vacuum lines or leaving footprints? Why would she even try? It's her house."

"She couldn't have." The tech shifted from foot to foot excitedly. "Someone vacuumed after this woman died. Probably trying to get rid of any evidence he or she might have left." The tech snorted. "As if." She looked to Detective Francois. "Can I get started?"

"Yes, and you heard the man." Francois sighed. "Lots of photos and be careful. This is shaping up to be a homicide."

MAGGIE OPENED THE front door and let Kevin and Detective Francois into her small home. She'd fallen in love with the cottage the moment she'd stepped into the house. The gleaming hardwood floors, soaring ceiling and wall of windows looking out of the back onto a sea of green grass had sold her on the place. Kim had helped her make a fresh start when she'd been convinced her life was over.

And now her friend was gone. Maggie beat back another crying jag. She'd already indulged in a good one while waiting for Kevin and Detective Francois to come for her.

She waved the men to the sofa. "I've made coffee. Can I get either of you a cup?"

"Please." Detective Francois smiled.

"None for me," Kevin answered.

"Still not a coffee drinker, I see." A faint smile crossed her lips. He'd always said it tasted like liquified mud when they were in college.

"Never acquired a taste for it." Kevin smiled back.

It only took a moment to pour two cups of coffee, one for the detective and another for herself. She arranged the cups, a small carafe of cream and a sugar bowl on a tray and carried it into the living room. She settled the coffee on the table beside the sofa and took her cup to the only other seat in the room, a blue easy chair she'd found at the Salvation Army that had still been in good shape. Or at least good enough shape.

Detective Francois took a long sip of coffee.

Maggie held the cup in her hand, staring at the dark liquid inside but not drinking. "Kim is dead." She didn't need confirmation of that. "How?"

"We are very much still in the preliminary stages of the investigation." The detective set the mug aside and pulled out his cell phone. "Can you take me through what happened from the time you and Mr. Lombard left the museum?"

Maggie let out a shuddering breath and began. Kevin remained quiet while she recounted their steps from the museum to finding Kim, but she could tell he'd already gone through the story with Detective Francois.

"Did Ms. Sumika do drugs?" Detective Francois asked.

Maggie jolted at the detective's question. How could he know? She shook her head. "No. Not anymore. She'd been clean for years. A decade."

Francois pinned Maggie in his gaze. "But she used to do drugs."

Maggie hesitated.

"I know you might not want to say something that could paint Kim in a bad light," Kevin said, "but anything you can tell the detective could help to figure out exactly what happened here."

"Kim didn't do drugs." Maggie believed that despite what she'd seen when they'd found her friend's body. "Not anymore. She had a problem when she was an undergraduate. Before we met. She dropped out of college for a while, but she went into rehab, and she was clean by the time we met in grad school, although she was up-front about her addiction."

"I believe you," Kevin said.

She searched his face and found nothing, but he seemed sincere. Unfortunately, she couldn't say the same about Detective Francois's expression. To say he appeared skeptical was an understatement.

"Do you know where or from whom she got her drugs?" Detective Francois asked.

She gritted her teeth. "I don't. I told you that was before we met. I wouldn't have moved in here if I didn't believe that she'd conquered that demon."

Detective Francois stopped typing the note he'd been putting in his phone. "What do you think happened then?"

Maggie stayed silent. That was the question, wasn't it? She thought Kim had beat her addiction, but relapses among addicts weren't uncommon. She'd been busy planning for the opening and the Viperé exhibit. Maybe she'd missed the signs. Maybe she'd failed her friend. Or maybe there hadn't been any signs because Kim hadn't relapsed. Maybe her overdose wasn't an accident. Maybe it was murder. But that was just too hard to comprehend.

"I don't know." It wasn't satisfactory for anyone, but it was the only answer she could give the detective.

"We'll have to wait for the medical examiner's report to be sure, but the scene has all the signs of an overdose, and at the moment, we are proceeding as if it is such. We will of course explore every avenue and go wherever the evidence takes us," Detective Francois said.

He moved on. "Did Ms. Sumika do her own housework?"

The sudden change in subject threw Maggie. "Housework?"

"Yes, you know." The detective waved the phone as he spoke. "Laundry. Cooking. Doing the dishes. Cleaning. Vacuuming."

She had no idea why that information would be relevant to Kim's death but wanted to do anything she could to help the detective. "No. She had a service come in twice a week."

"Huh. Sounds expensive," Francois remarked. "I don't expect that she would have made the kind of money to afford the house, a twice-a-week cleaning service, and I saw a very nice Audi Sport in the garage."

Maggie let out a frustrated breath. Kim shouldn't be the one on trial. She was a victim. "Kim came from money. The house was her childhood home. She inherited it when her parents died a couple years ago within months of each other. A real love story."

Maggie had been almost as devastated as Kim when,

first, Kim's mother had passed then, two months later, her father, both from heart attacks, although Kim believed her father's had been brought on from the devastating loss of his soulmate.

"Ah, well that makes sense then."

Kevin cleared his throat, drawing the attention in the room to him. "Was Kim right- or left-handed?"

"Oh…" Another question out of left field. "She was right-handed. Why?"

The men shared a look, but neither answered her.

That wasn't going to do for her. She stood. "Look, I want to help. I want to know what happened to Kim, and if someone…" She swallowed the sob that bubbled in her throat. "And if someone hurt her, I want them brought to justice more than anyone. I can help you."

Both men stood.

"You are helping," Detective Francois said. "By answering my questions."

She shot a glance at Kevin and then back at Francois. "You're letting him into the investigation. Why not me?"

"Mr. Lombard is a former police officer and trained security specialist."

And Kevin wasn't a suspect in a major jewel theft. The detective didn't say that, but Maggie had no problem hearing it in the silence that fell. She had a feeling she was going to get good at hearing the things Francois didn't say.

Detective Francois tucked his phone into his suit pocket. "It's been a long night. We'll go and let you get some sleep, but I'll likely have more questions for you in the coming days. About the theft and Ms. Sumika."

She crossed her arms over her torso and followed the men to the front door.

Detective Francois stepped into the night, headed to the Tudor without a glance back.

Kevin stopped on her small front stoop. "Hey, he's right about one thing. You've been through more than any one person should have to deal with in one night. Try to get some rest. Maybe call a friend to come stay with you."

Maggie shook her head and finally let the tears she'd been holding back fall. She met his gaze, surprised to find sympathy there. "Rest isn't what's going to help me get through this. Helping to find Kim's killer will."

Chapter Five

Kevin arrived at police headquarters just after ten the next morning. Tess had set up a status meeting for them with Detective Francois. His boss had been busy in the hours since he'd seen her last. The Larimer Museum's insurance company had agreed to employ West Investigations to find the Viperé jewel, although Tess had stressed that the working relationship was tenuous. West's reputation had taken a hit with the theft, but they had a longstanding relationship with this particular insurance company, and that had gone a long way in convincing them to allow West to take the first crack at the case.

The Los Angeles Police Department had also agreed to let West work with them. They had more than enough to deal with without adding a jewel heist to their ever-growing list of investigations. They'd still take the lead with respect to Kim Sumika's possible homicide, but Kevin would work with Detective Francois on the jewel theft and have full access to the detective. Kevin was surprised Tess had been able to pull off such access, and she'd admitted that his prior experience as a police officer had helped her convince the powers that be in the LAPD to let him help. Despite the show of faith from the insurance company and the police departments, both he and

Tess knew that the reputation of West's new West Coast office was on the line.

He gave his name to the young officer who sidled up to the bulletproof glass separating the clerk's desk from the public. After showing his identification and going through the metal detectors, he took a precarious ride on a rickety elevator to the fourth floor.

The elevator doors opened onto a depressingly gray hallway where Detective Francois and Tess waited.

"Sorry. Am I late?" Kevin said, stepping out of the elevator.

"Not at all," Detective Francois answered. He held a black leather folio in one hand. "Tess was on her way up when I got the call that you were right behind her, so we figured we'd just wait and take the walk to the conference room together."

Detective Francois started off down the hallway. Kevin and Tess followed closely behind. The detective waved them into a small conference room at the end of the hall. He offered water and coffee, which Kevin and Tess declined. They settled in around the conference table, Francois pulling out his phone while Tess pulled out a tablet. Kevin went old school with his trusty lined notebook.

"The lab is still running tests on the evidence collected from the Sumika scene, but the medical examiner was able to give me a preliminary time of death, 10:04 p.m."

Tess wore a questioning expression. "That's unusually specific for a time of death."

Francois read from his phone. "We lucked out there. Ms. Sumika's watch was also one of those heartbeat, pulse thingies. We were able to get the exact time her pulse and heartbeat went to zero."

"Lucky for us. Not so lucky for Kim Sumika," Tess said.

Kevin noted the timing. "That is about forty minutes before Maggie Scott and the guard at the Larimer were attacked."

Francois nodded. "Give or take."

Tess's gaze bounced between the two men. "Just so we are all on the same page, everyone here is suspicious of the timing of the theft and Ms. Sumika's death. I mean, I know we don't have a definitive ruling of homicide—"

"Yet—" Kevin said because he wasn't just suspicious. He'd thought about it all last night, and it was too convenient to believe that the assistant curator just happened to overdose on the very night a priceless jewel was stolen from the museum where she worked.

"It's hard to believe they are unrelated," Tess continued.

Francois shifted in his chair. "It seemed unlikely, but we have to keep an open mind and explore all possibilities."

"Of course," Tess said without conviction.

"I pulled background and credit checks on Kimberly Sumika, Maggie Scott, Carl Downy and Robert Gustev." Francois pulled several sheets of paper from his folio and slid them across the table to Tess and Kevin.

"Did you go home at all last night?" Tess joked.

"No," Francois answered seriously.

The detective was dedicated. Kevin respected that.

"Scott, Downy and Gustev all look clean, but Sumika has run up quite a bit of debt."

Kevin flipped to Kim's financials. Francois wasn't joking about the amount of debt. Nearly three hundred fifty thousand dollars' worth.

"Maggie said that Kim had an inheritance from her parents. How did she get into so much debt?" Kevin asked.

"It looks like the inheritance was limited to the house, which to be fair, in this market isn't paltry," Tess said, reading through the packet Francois had given them.

She cocked her head to the side, thinking. "But a house isn't liquid. Getting cash out would require taking a mortgage or selling."

"Exactly." Francois nodded. "It looks like Sumika maxed out her credit cards and a home equity line of credit."

Kevin frowned. That didn't make sense. "The house is worth a lot, but Kim didn't make the kind of money to pay that loan back. But why did she need that much money in the first place?"

Francois pointed a finger. "That's the three-hundred-fifty-thousand-dollar question."

"Maggie might know the answer," Kevin offered.

His thoughts had strayed to Maggie more than once during the night. She really should have gone to the hospital to have her head wound checked out. If she had a concussion, they could be tricky, and it didn't seem as if she had anyone to check up on her. His thoughts hadn't been exclusive to her health. He'd also wondered if she could have had anything to do with the theft of the Viperé ruby. At least, she couldn't have been involved with Sumika's death, not directly anyway. The time of death made that impossible.

"I plan on questioning her again today. Maybe she'll remember something helpful," Francois said.

"Do we think that Ms. Scott or the guard had a hand in the theft?" Tess asked.

Even though he'd been entertaining the idea himself, the knowledge that Tess and Detective Francois might also be considering it didn't sit well in Kevin's gut.

"I mean, we have to consider it," Tess added, though she couldn't have known how he was feeling.

"I'm definitely considering it." Francois frowned. "Ms. Scott's financials don't throw up any flags, but I find it strange that she works with and lives on the same property as our victim. Not to mention she also knew the code for the security system and knows how valuable the Viperé ruby is."

Tess propped her tablet up. "I downloaded the security footage from our server. We can see what happened up until the time the cameras were shut off."

Tess cued up the video, and the screen sprang to life. They watched Maggie enter the empty gallery and have a drink in front of the Viperé ruby. After a couple of minutes, she suddenly jerked as if something startled her then walked toward the hallway. The screen went black after that.

"Any footage of the guard's attack?" Francois asked.

Tess shook her head. "No cameras in the area where the security office is. None of the other cameras picked up anything or appeared to have been tampered with."

"So someone gets into the museum without being seen—"

"That might not have been difficult. The intruder could have come in during the donors' open house and hidden himself or herself until the party was over."

"It's as good a theory as any," Francois concurred. "But the intruder had to know that there weren't cameras in the hall leading to the security office and to hide there."

Kevin frowned. "If you're thinking about Maggie Scott, the timing doesn't work. The video we do have clearly shows her in the gallery with the ruby when the camera shuts off."

Francois's shoulders rose then fell. "Maybe she figured out a way to shut the camera off remotely. Or maybe she had help."

"Kim Sumika." Tess said what Francois had left unspoken.

Francois's shoulder went up and down again.

A protective instinct flared in Kevin's chest. That would not do. Francois was right to explore the possibility that Maggie Scott had something to do with the theft. The detective wouldn't be doing his job if he didn't. And neither would he if he ignored the possibility because he had a misplaced attraction to the pretty assistant curator.

"Maggie and Kim working together doesn't get around the timing issue," Kevin said, hoping his voice sounded nothing but professional. "Maggie couldn't have killed Kim, and if Kim was somehow involved with the theft, where is the ruby?"

"There could be a third player," Tess offered. "In fact, there is likely at least one other person involved whether or not Maggie Scott or Kim Sumika was. Whoever stole the ruby would need a fence to sell it."

"Maggie Scott probably knows a lot of people in the antiquities world, including dealers." Francois rubbed his chin.

"Everyone involved in this case probably knows art dealers. They are all involved in the art world," Kevin growled.

"Point taken." If Francois noticed the tone in his voice, he kept it to himself. "Still, I think that reaching out to the local dealers is a good idea."

"Me too," Tess said.

"Agreed," Kevin rumbled. "We also have to consider that the jewel wasn't stolen in order to be sold."

Francois tapped his phone screen. "That someone stole it because of the legend and dispute surrounding it."

"Exactly," Kevin said. "I did a little research of my own last night after leaving Maggie Scott's place, and there are very passionate groups on both sides of the issue. The government of Isle Bení has been in litigation with the British government for decades arguing that the jewel should be returned to the people of the island. So far, they've been unsuccessful."

"Someone could have gotten tired of waiting and decided to take matters into their own hands." Tess spun the tablet around and closed its cover. "But it's not as if they could just give the ruby back to the Bení government."

"No," Kevin agreed, "but it wouldn't stop them from returning the jewel to the island. The general public might not know it was there, but if the thief is a true believer, they may not care. The ruby being back on the island may be the goal, not public acknowledgment that it is there."

"So, we have two possible theories right now," Francois summed up. "One, the ruby could have been stolen to sell it."

"Or two," Tess picked up the detective's line of thought, "it could have been stolen by someone who believes in the legend and wants to return it to what they believe is its proper place on the island."

"We still have more questions than answers," Kevin said, looking from Francois to Tess, "but one thing that seems to be clear is that Maggie Scott is in the middle of whatever this thing is."

Chapter Six

The next day dawned bright and clear, and if she didn't look out of the cottage's front windows, Maggie could pretend that it was just another ordinary day. But when she inevitably did look, she could see the yellow crime scene tape still strung around the perimeter of Kim's Tudor, and the events of the night before washed out any fantasy she might have had.

The Viperé ruby was still missing, and Kim was dead. And she was a suspect in both crimes if she'd read Detective Francois and Kevin correctly.

That was more than enough to make anyone want to hide in bed indefinitely, but she couldn't. She wasn't sure whether the police would allow them back into the Larimer so soon, but Colin Rycroft, director of the London Natural History Museum, the museum that had loaned the Viperé ruby to the Larimer, would be in town that afternoon for a private tour of the exhibit. She hadn't spoken to Mr. Gustev since the night before, but surely he would have notified Rycroft and the London Natural History Museum of the theft by now.

She had switched on the television as soon as she'd awoken that morning, and there'd been a short segment on the break-in, although thankfully no mention of exactly what had been stolen. Rycroft was sure to be apoplectic about the missing Viperé, and the Larimer's reputation in the community would be ruined. They might never convince another museum to agree to an exchange again.

She'd just finished showering and dressing when her phone rang. Boyd Scott's gruff, smiling face filled the screen.

It had been several weeks since she'd spoken to her father. She knew her father loved her. He'd been a single parent since his beloved wife, her mother, died when she was ten. It had been a crushing blow to father and daughter. Boyd had dealt with losing his wife by entering into a series of short-term, ill-fated marriages that had led to them moving around the country a lot. In her sophomore year of high school, they'd moved to Los Angeles, Boyd's sixth wife's hometown. The marriage was over by the start of her senior year, but she convinced her father to stick it out in the city until she graduated. He'd made it a whole week after her graduation before taking off. These days, her father generally only called when he needed something from her, usually money. Her father's itinerant lifestyle hadn't exactly laid the foundation for a stable, well-funded retirement.

But she couldn't help hoping that this time was different. That her father had heard about the robbery at the Larimer and that he was calling now for no other reason than to make sure his only daughter was safe.

She answered the call.

"Hi, sweetheart," her father said cheerfully. "How's my favorite girl?"

"Tired. I didn't get much sleep last night, and today isn't likely to be any better."

"Oh?" A note of surprise sounded in her father's voice.

"That's too bad. It's important to get the proper amount of sleep."

So this call wasn't to check on her. Her father had no idea about her assault at the Larimer or the stolen ruby.

She sighed. "I do my best, Dad. So what can I do for you?"

"Nothing. Why do you always assume I'm calling you for something? Can't a father call his daughter just to check in on her?"

A father could, but her father didn't. But she kept that thought to herself. She was in no mood for an argument.

"Sorry, Dad. Like I said, I didn't get a lot of sleep."

"It's okay, sweetie. I won't keep you. I did have a little favor I wanted to ask you."

And there it was.

She loved her father. She really did. She wouldn't say her childhood was stable or financially secure, but she'd never worried about having a roof over her head or food on the table. Her father had always been there for her, helping her with homework, showing up at every performance the semester she was in the school play, and coming home every night even when she might have wished he'd pull an extra shift or two just to have a bit of savings in the bank.

But that was just it. Boyd Scott didn't believe in saving. "You can't take it with you" was his favorite saying. And to her father that saying was a license to spend, spend, spend. He spent money as fast as he made it, which often led to the need to borrow money from his daughter in order to deal with those pesky obligations like rent, electricity and car insurance, to name a few bills she'd forked over money to cover in the last year. She knew she should refuse. As long as her father knew she'd be there as a safety net, he'd never get his own financial house in order, but it was hard to say no to Boyd Scott. As evidenced by his six wives.

"How much do you need?" she asked, resigned to their respective roles in this scene.

"Nothing," he said with a touch of indignation in his voice that almost made her laugh. "I don't need any money." He took a pregnant pause. "I got engaged."

Maggie sat down hard in the chair at her kitchen table. She'd figured her father's days of getting hitched were over. It had been sixteen years since his divorce from wife number six, and while he'd had a few serious-for-him relationships since then, they hadn't ended in marriage. She knew it was immature; her father was only fifty-nine, hardly an old man, but...*ewww.*

She stifled her first reaction and instead said, "Engaged?"

"I know it's a shock. It was a surprise to me too. Well, not a surprise, I've been seeing Julie for nine months now."

She vaguely remembered her father mentioning a girlfriend in one of their prior calls, but honestly, she'd stopped attempting to remember his girlfriends' names long ago. *Julie.* It didn't ring a bell.

"We took a weekend getaway to Vegas, and one thing led to another, bing bang boom, I'm going to be a married man. Again."

Again.

"I..." Maggie wasn't sure what to say. Her father married again on top of everything else was too much to process, so her mind just didn't. "Congratulations, Dad."

"Thanks, baby. Now about that favor I mentioned. I want you and Julie to meet."

"Dad, now is not a good time. I…"

"Maggie, it doesn't have to be today, but soon. I want my two best girls to get to know each other. I know you and Julie are going to love each other. As much as I love you both."

The doorbell rang, saving her from having to come up with an answer right away.

"Dad, there's someone at my door. I'll call you back."

"Okay." She noted the hint of disappointment in her father's voice, guilt flooding through her. "Hey, sweetie. I love you."

"I love you too, Dad. I'll call soon, and we'll set something up."

She ended the call and went to the door.

Lisa stood on the stoop with a to-go cup in each hand. "Open up!"

Maggie swung the door open. "What are you doing here?"

Lisa pushed her way into the house and threw her arms around Maggie, careful not to spill as she did. "What am I doing here?" she said, pulling back. "I wake up to a text that says, 'Theft at the museum. I'm banged up but fine. Call you later,' and you think I'm not going to come and check on you? What kind of bestie do you think I am?"

Maggie grinned. "You are the best bestie there is."

She and Lisa had met not long after Lisa moved to Los Angeles at an event at the Getty. Maggie had never found it particularly easy to make friends, especially as she'd gotten older, but Lisa Eberhard was a force to be reckoned with. She'd been admiring the painting *Portrait of a Woman* when Lisa had walked up and begun rattling off the history of the painting and the Dutch artist who'd painted it, Jan Mytens. She'd learned that Lisa was a writer, a ghostwriter to be exact, and that she had the same love and appreciation of art that Maggie recognized in herself. She'd walked the rest of the exhibit with Lisa then they'd gone for coffee. It had been an instant connection, and they'd been friends ever since.

"Damned straight." Lisa thrust one of the to-go cups at Maggie. "Dark roast. Figured you'd need strong stuff today."

Maggie took the cup and sipped. "You figured right."

"What's with the caution tape around Kim's house? Is she doing renovations again?" Lisa asked, settled in on the sofa in her usual spot.

Maggie sat. Kim and Lisa were cordial, but they'd never really taken a liking to each other. Still, it hadn't seemed right to mention Kim's death in the text she'd sent to Lisa last night. She'd planned to call her friend and catch her up on everything that had happened later that day.

"Lisa, Kim overdosed last night. She's…gone."

Lisa sat stunned for a moment. "Overdosed? But I thought she'd kicked her habit a long time ago."

"I don't know what happened." She felt tears welling in her eyes.

"Oh, honey." Lisa set her cup on the coffee table and scooted forward on the sofa so she could wrap Maggie in a hug. "I'm so sorry."

Maggie let herself cry on her friend's shoulder for a minute before straightening. "It doesn't make any sense. Kim was clean. I know she was. This whole thing, the theft, Kim's death, it's like the world has gone crazy. None of it makes sense."

Lisa studied Maggie while she sipped her coffee. "Maggie, are you really okay? You know you can come and stay with me for a while. Or I can stay with you."

"I love you for offering, but we're going to be all hands on deck at the museum dealing with the fallout of the theft and Kim's death."

"You can't possibly be thinking about going into work today?"

"I have to. At least, if the museum is open. The director of the museum who loaned us the Viperé is scheduled for a private walk-through of the exhibit."

Lisa made a face. "Yikes."

"Exactly. I'd planned to call Mr. Gustev at nine thirty to find out what he wanted to do."

"If you are going to work, what are you planning to do with that black eye?"

Maggie touched two fingers to her eye. It was still tender. "I tried to cover it."

Lisa made another face. "You did not succeed."

"It looks worse than it is."

"It looks pretty bad."

It did. She'd tried to cover the worst of it with makeup, but that had only seemed to make the purplish bruise stand out more.

Lisa stood abruptly. Everything Lisa did had an abrupt quality about it. She was one of those people who vibrated with energy even when she was standing still. "Where's your makeup kit? I'll see what I can do with it."

Maggie did all right with her day-to-day makeup, but Lisa was a wiz at makeup. She had the patience for layering, blending and whatever else professional makeup artists did that made a face full of products look barely there.

She followed her friend into the bathroom and sat down on the closed toilet seat while Lisa rifled around in her makeup bag, lamenting the slim pickings.

"Ah-ha." Lisa turned with concealer in one hand and foundation in the other. "Now tell me all about last night."

Maggie did as Lisa asked while she did her best to cover her black eye. As a ghostwriter, Lisa had penned books for a handful of celebrities as well as a few politicians. She was good at what she did, and one of the many skills she'd developed from working with recalcitrant rich people was a knack for interrogation without seeming to be prying. By the time she'd finished covering the worst of the shiner, she'd pulled the whole story, detail by excruciating detail, from Maggie. By the end of the tale, though, Maggie felt marginally better.

"Ta-da." Lisa pulled Maggie to her feet and over to the bathroom mirror.

She could see a dark ring around her eye, but it looked more like she'd had a rough night and less like she'd been in a cage match.

"Thank you."

The doorbell rang.

Lisa's brow arched. "Expecting someone?"

She wasn't. She and Lisa walked to the front door together. Maggie looked out the peephole while Lisa went to the front widow and pulled back the curtain.

Kevin Lombard stood on the front stoop, a to-go cup and white paper bag in one hand.

Lisa let the curtain drop and shot her friend a crooked grin. "Girlfriend, have you been holding out on me?"

MAGGIE OPENED THE door to Kevin. "What are you doing here?"

He held up the coffee and bag. "I came to check on you. And I brought breakfast. Can I come in?"

Maggie hesitated for a moment before moving aside to let him cross the threshold.

Lisa cleared her throat, still standing by the window. Kevin spun in her direction.

"Hello, I'm Lisa, Maggie's best friend. And you are?"

Kevin quirked a brow. "Kevin Lombard."

"He's the security expert I told you about. With the firm that provides security for the Viperé ruby."

Lisa tsked. "You guys are in a spot of trouble then." She ambled to the sofa and slung her purse over her shoulder. "I have to go. I have a meeting with a prospective client that I can't reschedule, but if you need me to, I can come back this evening. Stay the night. We can have an old-fashioned sleepover."

Maggie wrapped her arms around her friend and pulled her into a tight hug. "I'll be fine. I'll call you tonight."

"You better," Lisa said, stepping back and heading for the door. "Bye, Kevin Lombard."

"I'm glad to see you asked a friend to stay with you," Kevin said after the door closed behind Lisa.

"I didn't actually call." Maggie turned and walked to her small kitchen, sitting at the table. "Lisa just showed up."

"The sign of a true friend," Kevin said, sitting across the table from her. He slid the coffee and bag to her. "It's a blueberry muffin. I don't know what you like, but who doesn't like blueberry muffins?"

"Thank you." She pushed the coffee to the side, it was too soon for a second cup, but she did like blueberry muffins. She pulled the muffin from the bag. "You didn't get yourself anything."

"I had a muffin on my way here."

"So—" she swiped her hands together, dusting off crumbs "—why are you here?"

"I have a few more questions I'm hoping you can answer."

"Why isn't Detective Francois asking the questions?"

Kevin frowned. "The LAPD has agreed to allow West Investigations to work with them on this case. Specifically, looking into the jewel theft. Detective Francois has enough on his plate looking into your friend's death."

Despite feeling more exhausted than she'd ever been in her life, she'd barely slept all night, thinking about the ruby and Kim. The two situations had to be connected. Had the thieves killed Kim? But if so, why?

"I can call Detective Francois if you'd be more comfortable speaking to him?" Kevin said, pulling her attention back to the present.

"No, it's fine. What did you want to ask me?"

"I'm sure Detective Francois asked you this last night, but can you think of anyone who had a grudge against the Larimer or anyone who took an unusual interest in the ruby?"

"Actually, Detective Francois did ask me that question already, but I was in such a daze last night—"

"Shock," he offered. "You'd just been through a scary and traumatizing experience."

She hugged her arms around her middle. "That's for sure. I told Detective Francois that I couldn't think of anyone who'd steal the ruby, but that's not true. At least, I don't think they would go so far as to steal the ruby, but…"

Kevin pulled a small notebook from his pocket. "Who are they?"

"The Art and Antiquities Repatriation Project."

Kevin laughed. "AARP? Really?"

Maggie held her hands up, palms out, a smile tipping her lips. "Hey, I didn't name the group. They're a nonprofit that works to return art and other cultural artifacts back to their countries of origin."

"And they had a problem with the Larimer Museum?"

She nodded. "They have a problem with a lot of museums. They were upset that we were hosting the Viperé exhibit. They staged a protest outside the museum a few weeks ago. But, like I said, they're a passionate group but reputable. I don't think they'd break the law. At least, not this way."

Kevin jotted something in his notebook. "You never know how far people will go if they feel they don't have any other choice. I'll check them out. Let's change focus for a moment. Assume that the thief doesn't want to repatriate the ruby but wants to sell it instead. How would they go about doing that?"

Maggie shook her head. "That wouldn't be easy. You can't just take a well-known, stolen gem to a pawnshop and trade it in for cash."

"Of course not, but these things can be sold on the black market. We both know that."

"Are you asking me if I know any shady antiquities dealers who'd be willing to offload the Viperé ruby on the black market?"

"I'm sure you and the Larimer only do business with reputable dealers, but you are in this industry. At this point, any lead would be helpful. Rumor. Speculation. Can you think of anyone who'd be willing to resort to theft to get the ruby?"

She shook her head again. "That might be a better question for Colin Rycroft."

She watched Kevin write the name in his notebook. "Colin Rycroft. Who is he?"

"He's the director of the London Natural History Museum. They loaned the ruby to the Larimer for the exhibit. Mr. Rycroft will be in town this afternoon. I can ask him if he'd be willing to speak with you."

Although, she was sure Colin Rycroft would be in no mood to do her or anyone affiliated with the Larimer any favors. But maybe in the interest of getting the Viperé back quickly, he'd agree to speak to Kevin. He'd almost certainly have to speak to Detective Francois.

"That would be helpful. Back to the dealers."

Maggie held up a hand. "I don't know any dealers who would risk their reputations, not to mention a lengthy jail sentence, to fence the ruby, but I will ask around. Maybe someone has heard something."

"Thank you again. You mentioned that the ruby is the subject of several lawsuits over ownership. Have any of the parties involved in the lawsuits contacted you? Maybe someone was upset enough about the exhibit to go to extremes."

"We had a few emails and phone calls from people expressing disagreement with the museum's decision to feature the ruby in an exhibit given the disputes over provenance and expatriation."

"Did you keep a list of those names?"

She shook her head. "I didn't, but I could probably generate one."

"That would be very helpful."

Maggie chewed her bottom lip. "Can I ask you something?"

"Sure."

"Why were you and Detective Francois asking all those

questions about Kim's cleaning habits and whether she was right- or left-handed?"

Kevin hesitated.

"Kim was my friend," Maggie pressed. "I deserve answers."

"There are some indications that Ms. Sumika may not have voluntarily overdosed."

Her mouth went dry. "Are you saying Kim was—"

"I'm not saying anything other than that Detective Francois's investigation is ongoing and he's investigating all possibilities."

She wasn't sure what to do with the information he'd just dropped on her. It was clear that he and Detective Francois at least suspected Kim's death might not be an accidental overdose, but if it wasn't... She wasn't sure she could deal with that blow on top of everything else.

Maggie balled up the now empty muffin wrapper. "Is there anything else?"

She still needed to call her boss and find out if going into the museum was possible, but Kevin didn't need to know that.

"Just one more thing," he said, looking up from his notebook. "Detective Francois pulled Ms. Sumika's finances, and it appears that she was in serious debt."

"No." He had to be wrong. "Kim never mentioned anything about being in debt. Her parents passed, so I don't know the particulars about her inheritance, but I got the feeling her parents left her a substantial amount."

"It appears she inherited the house free and clear, but there was very little money. She took out a mortgage on the house, and combined with her credit card debt, she owed more than three hundred thousand dollars."

"Three hundred—" she sputtered "—thousand?"

"It looks that way. You don't have any idea what the money was for or where it went?"

She had an idea of where the money could have gone, but it was just speculation, and she wasn't sure she wanted to share it with him, not yet at least. "She did some renovations to the house."

Kevin's eyes narrowed on her. He was shrewd. A former cop? She could see him in a uniform. Warmth flowed through her. Even with everything that had happened the night before, it hadn't escaped her notice how attractive he was. His penetrating dark gaze, athletic body and full beard was hard not to notice.

"Maggie," Kevin said, pulling her from her thoughts of him. "Holding back is only going to make it that much more difficult to find the ruby."

And possibly Kim's killer, although Kevin stopped short of saying that. But she was sure he didn't believe the ruby's theft and Kim's death were unconnected.

She sighed, reluctant to share her friend's confidences with Kevin if it would help them find Kim's killer. "Kim had a problem with gambling."

"Gambling."

"Kim was a good woman, but everyone has their troubles. Kim had an addictive personality. She kicked the drugs, but she replaced that habit with online gambling." Maggie rose, gathering the trash from the breakfast Kevin had bought her and tossing it into the trash can. Even though Kim was gone, it felt too much like she was betraying her friend.

"It started off small, just some online stuff." She leaned against the kitchen counter, wrapping her arms around herself. "I know Kim's parents helped her pay off an earlier debt about a year before they passed away. I had no idea she'd fallen back into that vice again."

It seemed there was a lot she didn't know about Kim even though they'd been living only footsteps apart for the last two years. How had she been so blind? Guilt swam in her chest. She hadn't been a good friend.

Kevin's pen scratched over the paper. "Three hundred thousand is a lot to spend online. Did she gamble anywhere else?"

She felt her face twist into a scowl. "She had a bookie. I haven't seen him around in years, so I don't know if they still communicated but…"

"It's a place to start. Do you remember the bookie's name?"

Maggie pushed away from the counter and stepped back to the table. "I do."

Kevin's eyebrow quirked up. "Will you share it with me?"

She shook her head. "No." She owed Kim more than that. She'd been her friend, and when she'd needed her, Maggie had failed her. She wanted to have a hand in bringing the person who'd hurt Kim to justice.

"No?"

"No, I won't tell you Kim's bookie's name, but I will take you to him."

Chapter Seven

Kevin did his best to get Maggie to let him talk to Kim's bookie on his own, but she wouldn't budge. He'd finally given in, and now he was following the directions barked out by his GPS system to the address Maggie had given him. At least the address was in the NoHo Arts District, a North Hollywood neighborhood, and not in a seedier area of town where Kevin would have assumed a bookie would reside.

Maggie called her boss as he drove them across town. The call wasn't on speaker phone, but he could hear both sides of the conversation easily. The police were planning to release the crime scene at noon, and although the museum wouldn't open to the public for at least several more days, Robert Gustev wanted to meet with the staff that afternoon. Colin Rycroft's tour of the exhibit was still on. Apparently, the director of the museum that lent the Viperé ruby to the Larimer was insisting on seeing the scene of the crime with his own eyes.

Miraculously, he found a parking spot on the street a half a block from the address Maggie had given him just as she ended her call.

This area of Los Angeles had undergone a renaissance in the last couple of decades. New shops and businesses had sprung up almost as fast as the rehabbed condos and apartments that had been bought and rented by hip millennials and Gen Zers.

Maggie strode ahead of him on the sidewalk, reaching for the door of a redbrick building in the middle of the block of buildings that housed various shops and businesses.

Kevin pulled up short. "Are you sure this is the right place?"

The sign above the door Maggie reached for read The Cupcake Bar.

She shot a grin at him over her shoulder. "Trust me. This is it."

He followed her through the doors. It was obvious that at some point this place had actually been a bar. The space was a mixture of light and dark: wide pine plank floors, dark red exposed brick walls and a long oak bar that ran the length of one side. The front of the bar had been retrofitted into a glass-fronted display case for the cupcakes inside. Behind the bar was a mirrored wall, but instead of the expected shelves of various and sundry liquors, the shelves were also lined with cupcakes.

The shop was empty, but the bell tinkling as they walked in brought a man in a pink apron with Cupcake Bar emblazoned on it through the swinging doors behind the bar.

"Good morning. Welcome to the Cupcake Bar. How may I help—" The clerk's gaze moved from Kevin to Maggie. "Oh, Maggie, it's you."

"Anthony, we need to talk to you," Maggie said.

Anthony's eyes moved back to Kevin, sliding over him appraisingly. "Who is *we*?"

Kevin stuck his hand out. "Kevin Lombard. My firm

has been hired to provide security at the Larimer Museum. Maggie and I have a few questions for you about Kim Sumika."

Anthony gave his hand a brief shake and sighed. "Maggie, you know I can't talk to you about my business with Kim."

"Anthony, Kim is dead."

Anthony's eyes went wide, and his mouth fell open. "What? How?"

"She was found last night, or this morning I guess. It looks like she accidentally overdosed, but—" Maggie shot a questioning glance at Kevin, her eyes asking how much she could tell Anthony.

He should have briefed her on what to say and not to say before they'd entered. Interviewing a witness could be a tricky business. Asking the right questions but doing so without leading the person in any particular direction was a learned skill. It was too late now.

He jumped into the conversation before Maggie said too much. "The police are still investigating. Maggie says you and Kim were…friends. We were wondering if you'd seen any signs that she was using again?"

Anthony looked confused. "If you work security for the Larimer, why are you asking me questions about Kim's death?"

"Because the Larimer was also robbed yesterday," Maggie answered.

"Damn." Anthony walked around the bar to one of the tables and sat.

Kevin and Maggie took seats across from him.

"A very precious ruby was stolen, and a guard and I were attacked," Maggie continued.

"Damn. I'm sorry to hear that. So you think Kim's

death is connected to the theft? It would be quite a coincidence if it wasn't, I guess." Anthony answered his own question.

"As I said, the police are exploring every possibility. My firm, West Investigations, is helping with the investigation into the theft," Kevin said. "So, about Kim's possible drug use."

Anthony gave a wan smile. "If Maggie brought you here, I'm sure she would have told you about my relationship with Kim. We weren't friends, not in the traditional sense."

"She told me you are Kim's bookie."

Anthony's shoulders went back, and he stayed silent.

"Okay." Kevin held up his hand. "During your nontraditional friendship, did you notice any signs that Kim might be using again?"

Anthony cocked his head to the side and thought for a moment. "I can't say I did, but I only saw Kim for short stretches of time. She'd come in, grab a cupcake, maybe a little something else—" he looked away guiltily "—and leave."

Kevin sighed. The whole baker-bookie thing was cute, an innovative way to stay under the radar, but he was investigating a theft and possible murder. He didn't have time for cuteness. "Look, man. I'm not a cop. I don't care about your bookmaking business unless it led to Kim Sumika's death. I just want some answers."

Anthony's expression hardened.

Maggie reached across the table for the clerk's hand. "Anthony, I know we haven't always seen eye to eye. I don't like your side hustle. I don't like what it did to Kim, but this is bigger than all that. There's a chance…" She shot a glance at Kevin, and he gave a slight nod. Sometimes giving a little led to getting a lot. He suspected this was one of those times. "A good chance Kim didn't accidentally overdose. That someone set it up to look like she did."

Anthony pulled his hand from Maggie's grasp, his expression incredulous. "You can't possibly be suggesting it was me?"

"Was it?" Kevin pressed.

"No. Of course not!"

Maggie straightened in her seat. "Kim was in a lot of debt."

"She'd been placing a lot of bets lately that didn't pan out, sure, but I wouldn't kill anyone over that. Most of my clients aren't good gamblers. It's how I stay in business."

"People have been killed for a lot less than three hundred thousand dollars."

"What?" Anthony stood so quickly his chair fell over backward. "Three hundred thousand. Uh, uh. No way. Kim didn't owe me anywhere near that amount of money."

"Sit," Kevin directed. He waited for Anthony to right his chair and reclaim his seat. "How much did she owe you?"

"A couple thousand. Look around, man. You think I'd be slinging cupcakes if I had three hundred thousand dollars to front one person? I'd be in Tahiti or something."

Kevin believed him. Three hundred thousand was a lot of cupcakes. "Do you have any idea why Kim would be in that kind of debt?"

Anthony's eyes darted to the ceiling.

"Anthony, please," Maggie said.

Anthony sighed. "I'm small-time, okay? I did the bookmaking thing to earn enough money to open the shop, and I continued taking bets from a select number of clients after I opened, but it's not my main source of income, you know."

"Okay." Kevin wished the man would just come out and say whatever it was.

"She was obsessed, addicted to gambling. I've seen it before, and I tried to steer her away from getting in too deep but..." He shrugged.

"She started placing bets with another bookie," Kevin said, seeing where this was going.

Anthony nodded. "Yeah."

"Do you know who?"

Anthony's gaze strayed again. "I don't know for sure..."

"You have an idea," Maggie said. "Tell us."

"Look, like I said, I don't know for sure, but she did ask me about Ivan Kovalev."

"Russian mob?" Kevin didn't know the name. He hadn't been in Los Angeles long enough to get to know who the major players in the local underworld were, but the Russian mob had long tentacles in the US. And they weren't the kind of men you wanted to owe money.

Anthony shrugged then nodded. "When Kim asked me about Ivan, I warned her to steer clear."

Maggie was chewing her bottom lip again. "What exactly did Kim want with this Ivan person?"

"She wanted to know if I knew him. Could I make an introduction." Anthony twisted his hands in his apron. "To be clear, I don't. I stick to my small-time hustle and don't mess with those guys."

"Smart," Kevin said.

The bell on the door tinkled, and four women walked in, chatting.

Anthony stood. "Listen, I have to go. I don't know anything else that can help you. I hope you figure out what happened to Kim. She had her issues, but she was a nice woman."

Anthony headed for the bar display case to help the new customers.

Neither Kevin nor Maggie spoke until they were back in his car.

"Do you think Kim got involved with this Ivan person? Could he have killed her? Or had her killed?"

It was definitely a possibility, but he could see the idea was already weighing on Maggie.

He reached across the car and squeezed her hand. The electric currents that he'd felt the first time he'd touched her were back, even stronger.

"I think our talk with Anthony the baker slash bookmaker raised more questions than answers."

Chapter Eight

Kevin called Tess from the car as he drove toward the museum and updated her on what they'd learned from Anthony.

"Ivan has his hands in a number of pies in Los Angeles and beyond. He owns several seemingly legit businesses, including a bar in downtown Los Angeles. Nightingale's. Conducts his shadier business at night out of the party room."

"Think you can get a meeting with him?" Kevin asked.

"I'll see what I can do," Tess answered before ending the call.

"If we know this Ivan guy hangs out at Nightingale's, why don't we just go there tonight and ask to speak to him?"

"Because, *a*, you don't just drop in on a mobster. And, *b*, we are not going to talk to him." Kevin glanced across the car. "He's someone you should stay away from."

She rolled her eyes. "Are you planning to go to talk to him? Find out if he knew Kim and lent her money?"

"Maggie, listen to me. Ivan Kovalev, the people he probably works for, these are not men you want knowing you even exist. I'm not going to let you anywhere near them, do you understand?"

"Let me?"

He sucked in a deep breath then let it out slowly, which only infuriated her more.

"I didn't mean it that way. I'm just trying to protect you. We don't know what Kim got herself into, but it is starting to look very dangerous."

As if it hadn't been dangerous before now. She'd been clocked in the head, her friend was dead, likely murdered, and a precious historical jewel was missing. She hadn't exactly been living in Shangri-la.

They made the rest of the ride in silence. He pulled to a stop in front of the museum a few minutes after twelve thirty.

"I can come back and pick you up at the end of your workday if you'd like," he offered, stiffly.

"That's nice of you," she responded, already reaching for the door, "but I'll get a ride from a colleague or call an Uber."

She hopped out of the car and headed for the museum. It actually wasn't that far of a walk from the museum to her cottage. She'd made the walk before.

The police tape was gone from the front of the museum, and her employee identification, which doubled as a key card, opened the door to the employee entrance without any trouble.

Her head was still swirling with news that Kim might have gotten herself involved with mobsters. She was so caught up in her thoughts that she gave a startled scream when the door to the ladies' room swung open as she passed and Diyana Shelton stepped out.

"Oh my gosh, Maggie. I'm so sorry. I didn't mean to frighten you," Diyana said, a flush pinking her pale cheeks. Diyana was in the UCLA graduate art history program and interning at the Larimer for the semester.

"No, it was my fault," Maggie said, her hand still pressed to her racing heart. "I wasn't paying attention."

"How are you?" Diyana cocked her head to the side, her expression one of concern. The graduate student was pretty in a somewhat unconventional way. Dark brown eyes were set a little wide and her lips were thin lines, but her olive-colored skin was smooth as silk, and somehow the individual features worked together. "I heard you and Carl were here when the ruby was stolen and that the thief attacked you both." Her eyes strayed to Maggie's injuries. This close, Maggie had no doubt Diyana could see the results of her encounter with the thief clearly enough.

"I'm okay and, thank goodness, so is Carl. It's the museum I'm worried about." Maggie started walking again toward her office.

Diyana fell in step next to her. "You're right to be. The theft is huge. I mean, I'm not sure what Robert is going to do. I heard him talking to Colin Rycroft on the phone earlier, and it did not sound like a friendly conversation. How could this have happened?"

Maggie stopped in front of her office. She didn't usually mind Diyana's curiosity, but she was simply in no mood for it today.

"I don't know, but I'm sure the police will find out. I can't chat right now, Diyana. I have to get ready for the staff meeting. I'll see you there." She slid into her office, closing the door behind her firmly before a wave of guilt hit.

She'd been a little abrupt, possibly bordering on rude. Diyana didn't deserve that. She'd apologize after the meeting.

Remembering her promise to Kevin to reach out to the dealers she knew about the stolen Viperé ruby, she put a call in to several dealers, including her friend Apollo Bouras. She left him a message asking him to call her back as soon as he could. No doubt he and every other dealer in the Los Angeles area had already heard about the theft of the Viperé ruby, and they'd either want to stay as far away from her and the Larimer as possible given the situation or they'd call back quickly, eager to snatch up any crumb of gossip to spread.

Messages left, she got busy wading through the hundreds of emails she'd received overnight. Several were from colleagues at other museums asking if she was okay and wanting the skinny on the break-in. She'd respond to those later. More than a dozen were from news organizations, several from the same reporters. Interview requests. She deleted those without opening most of them. All too soon, it was time for the staff meeting.

She was surprised to find Carter Tutwilder, chairman of the Larimer's board of directors, standing in front of the room next to Robert.

"Come in, come in. Find a seat. Quickly please," Robert said, waving her inside.

Maggie grabbed the empty seat next to Diyana and shot the young woman what she hoped was an apologetic smile. Diyana smiled back wanly.

"Okay, before we get started with the meeting, Mr. Tutwilder wanted to say a few words."

"Thank you, Robert." Mr. Tutwilder buttoned his suit jacket. "I won't impose for long. I just wanted to acknowledge the heinous crime that has been perpetrated against the Larimer and those of us who love the museum. Of course, no one more than Maggie and Carl." Mr. Tutwilder extended a hand in her direction. "Maggie, the Larimer and the board stand behind you one hundred percent. Whatever you need, we're here for you."

"Thank you," she said, touched by the show of concern.

"As soon as things settle down, we'll also be planning a memorial for our colleague Kim Sumika. The board has made grief counselors available to anyone who feels they need to talk." Mr. Tutwilder turned back to Robert. "I'll hand things back over to you, Robert."

"Thank you, Carter."

A polite smattering of applause broke out as Mr. Tutwilder left the room.

"Okay," Robert said. "Let's get started."

Robert began the meeting with an update on Carl's condition. He was admitted to the hospital with a serious concussion, but the doctors expected him to make a full recovery. The doctors planned to release him from the hospital in a few days, but it might be a couple weeks before he was up to returning to the job. Then Robert turned to the theft of the Viperé ruby and did his best to set everyone's concerns at ease, although Maggie wasn't sure how much he accomplished. They all knew that the longer it took for the police to find the ruby, the worse things would get for the Larimer. And there was a fair chance that the ruby would never be found. It would be a coveted possession amongst the sordid world of private collectors, a notoriously secretive bunch of people who collected treasures that should rightly be seen by the masses. A lot of these extremely wealthy collectors didn't much care how they came into possession of items, just that they obtained them.

It was a short meeting. Maggie pulled Diyana aside before she left and apologized for her abrupt dismissal earlier.

"It's okay." Diyana smiled sweetly. "We're all under a huge amount of pressure right now."

Maggie returned the intern's smile. "Thank you for understanding."

"Maggie." Robert stepped up next to Maggie and Diyana. "I'd like to speak to you for a moment, please."

Diyana nodded and scurried from the conference room. All the other staff members had already left the room.

Robert gestured for her to sit and she did. He sat across from her, folding his hands on the table in front of him. She felt like a child being admonished by the principal. She smoothed the front of her slacks nervously. Was he going to fire her? He wouldn't. She wasn't responsible for the theft. She was a victim as much as the Larimer.

She sat silently, waiting for him to start.

"I'm glad to see you weren't hurt badly."

She tried for a smile and failed. "No. I'm fine."

"Good, I'm happy to hear that, although I have been thinking that it might be a good idea if you took a leave of absence."

"A leave of absence?"

So he wasn't firing her. At least, not yet. But a leave of absence was no consolation.

"Well, some time off, really. Vacation time."

"Vacation time? Now?" She was confused. It was quite possibly the worst time for her to take a vacation. With Kim…and the media storm around the theft. "Robert, what is this about?"

He sighed heavily. He looked as if he'd aged two decades in the last twelve hours. "The Larimer is under a tremendous amount of pressure at the moment. All eyes are on us with the theft and Ms. Sumika's untimely death. And well, there are already rumblings that Kim might have had something to do with the theft, and that's what led her to do—" Robert rolled his wrist "—what she did."

"You can't believe that! You worked with Kim for years. You know as well as I do how much she loved the Larimer."

Robert avoided meeting her gaze. "I have a hard time believing anyone associated with the Larimer would have committed such a heinous act, but the fact is someone did. And your relationship with Ms. Sumika—"

Maggie felt her back stiffen. "My relationship with Kim was that we were friends and coworkers."

His lips thinned. "Be that as it may, I have an obligation to look out for the best interests of the museum, and we simply cannot afford to have even a hint of impropriety at the moment."

"Impropriety—"

"I believe that it would be best for you to separate yourself from the Larimer, at least for a time." He stood as if that put an end to the conversation.

Maggie got to her feet as well. "Well, I have a contract, and I expect it to be honored. And if you try to fire me or force me to take vacation time, I have no problem taking my grievances up with the board of directors."

"Now, just a moment—" Robert held his hands out as if they might stop the onslaught of words coming his way.

Her heart pounded wildly. She'd been through this before when Ellison was charged with embezzling from his accounting firm. Guilty by association. She couldn't go through it again. "No, no moments. I will not let you suggest that I am somehow involved in the theft of the Viperé ruby."

"I never said—" he spoke quickly.

"You came close enough. And if I'm suddenly placed

on leave or taking a vacation, those same people who are rumbling about Kim maybe being involved with the theft will be rumbling about me next. I will not have my reputation impugned when I did nothing wrong."

"No one is saying you did anything wrong."

"Great." She flashed a smile at him that she was pretty sure looked more feral than friendly by the way he took three quick steps backward. "Good. Then I'll head back to my office. Mr. Rycroft should be here any minute, and I'm sure we both want to be prepared for that meeting. I'll see you soon."

She stepped out of the room and marched back to her office. Inside, she rested her back against the closed door, shaking from a combination of anger and adrenaline. It had felt good standing up for herself, but she knew if Robert really wanted her out, there wasn't much she could do to stop him. He had far more sway with the board members than she had, and they'd likely do whatever he suggested if it meant a chance at saving the Larimer's reputation. Even if it ruined hers.

She pulled herself together moments before the security guard on duty buzzed to say that Colin Rycroft had arrived. She let Robert know then picked Rycroft up from the reception desk.

The Brit was not happy.

She and Robert spent the next two hours walking Rycroft through the exhibit and explaining how the Viperé ruby's theft couldn't have been foreseen. Rycroft made them walk through the security measures they'd had in place three times, and he read them the riot act for the failure of the cameras. It would have been nice to have Tess or Kevin there to explain the security system in more detail, but neither she nor Robert had thought of it in time. And given Tess's disgust at the museum's decision not to go with her original plan for securing the ruby, they might have been better off without a representative from West Investigations. Rycroft insisted that they set up a meeting with the insurance company and West Security and Investigations to go over the steps that were being taken to recover the ruby. Of course, the Larimer had obtained an insurance policy on the Viperé, but Rycroft wasn't incorrect that money was poor consolation for a piece as rare as the Viperé.

Maggie promised to set up a meeting between the parties in the coming days and hoped that Kevin's and Tess's obvious experience and expertise might work to mollify the Brit at least a little.

By the time Rycroft finally left the museum and headed back to his hotel—he planned to be in town for the next several days—she was wiped. It wasn't quite five thirty, officially quitting time, so she headed back to her office with every intention of going home. All she wanted was a big glass of wine.

She knew the moment she entered her office that someone had been there. The air felt different. There was a slight chill to it. Maybe that was why she'd shivered as she'd stepped over the threshold.

Or maybe it was the blood-red envelope that lay, center stage, on her desk.

A get-well card probably. She was overreacting to a colleague's caring gesture.

She grabbed the envelope and slipped the piece of paper from it.

Her heart stuttered to a stop as she read then reread the words on the card.

Beware the Viperé curse. You are next to die.

Chapter Nine

Kevin stepped into his apartment, dropping his keys on the table next to the door. He still had a lot of work to do, but luckily West Investigations equipped each of their employees with a fully secure laptop so they were able to work from practically anywhere in the world.

But it didn't seem likely that he was going to get a lot of work done at the moment. The television in his living room blared.

"Tanya," he called from the doorway. He couldn't see his sister from the entrance, but this wasn't the first time he'd come home to find her camped out on his sofa, the television loud enough to wake the dead.

He slipped out of his shoes and padded into the living room. "Tanya," he yelled at the back of his sister's head.

Tanya turned and grinned at him over the back of the sofa. "Hey, bro."

People were always surprised when they found out he and Tanya were brother and sister and outright shocked when they found out they were twins. He was tall, six two and dark—dark brown hair, eyes and skin. Tanya, in contrast, was petite at five foot one, with skin the color of café latte, piercing hazel eyes and light brown hair streaked with blond. Two sides of the same coin their mother liked to call them, pointing out that where it really mattered they were very much alike. They were both driven, bossy, stubborn and thought they knew best. Kevin couldn't really dispute their mother's assessment. He and Tanya were very much alike, which tended to both draw them close and lead to a fair amount of arguing. But there was no one more loyal than Tanya, and he would do anything to protect his younger-by-seven-minutes sister.

Kevin dropped down on the sofa next to his sister. He didn't bother asking her what she was doing there. The red beans and rice she was shoveling into her mouth was all the answer he needed.

Tanya was an emergency room doctor at the nearby hospital, and given that she was still in her scrubs, her crocs lined up neatly by his front door, he inferred she'd come over directly at the end of her shift. When he'd announced he was leaving the Idyllwild Police Department and accepting a job with West Security and Investigations that would put him in Los Angeles and closer to her, Tanya had conveniently found him the perfect rental just minutes away from the hospital. Since the place had two bedrooms, he'd offered to let her move in with him, but she'd declined, saying that they needed their space. That hadn't stopped her from accepting the spare key he'd offered her and stopping in whenever she wanted, most often to bum leftovers off of him. He chided her about her visits, but the truth was he loved spending time with her. She was more than just his sister, she was his best friend.

"You look tired," she said, peeling her gaze away from the rerun of *The Office* playing on the television screen.

He put a hand to his ear and leaned toward her. "I'm sorry, I can't hear you. What did you say?" he yelled over the sound of the television.

She rolled her eyes but reached for the remote tucked under her legs and turned the volume down to something reasonable. "Better?"

"Yes, thank you. You know turning the sound up that loud isn't good for you."

"I wanted to hear the show while I was in the kitchen heating up dinner. You really outdid yourself, by the way. This is good." She shoveled more beans and rice into her mouth.

"You know, I seem to recall giving you the recipe for this dish. And showing you how to make it. And a few others. I know you are far more skilled in the emergency room than the kitchen, but for a smarty-pants doctor like you, red beans and rice can't be that hard to master," he teased.

"It's not hard to master," she said around a bite of food. "But you know what is easier? Coming over here and eating your food." She grinned at him again. "Anyway, you cook enough for a small army."

"I wonder why." He pulled the throw pillow from behind his back and tossed it at her before slouching down until his head rested against the back of the sofa.

Tanya shifted, crossing her legs on the sofa and facing him. "New job putting you through your paces?"

"I caught a particularly thorny case."

Tanya had gone to CalSci University with him and Maggie. Although they'd tried to give each other space to explore who they were outside of being Kevin's twin sister and Tanya's twin brother, Tanya had been there throughout his relationship with Maggie and had been there for him when he'd decided to end things with her. She'd even tried to talk him out of ending things, arguing that she could take out loans and work her way through medical school. But he hadn't wanted her to be burdened with the kind of debt that most medical students graduated with. He'd spent three years playing college football, making who knew how much money for the university, and he figured it was time that some of those big bucks benefited his mother and sister. Professional athletes were always on borrowed time, and he didn't want to waste any of his. So he'd left school after his junior year and directed his entire focus toward his NFL career. A career that, unbeknownst to him at the time, would only last for two years.

"Can you tell me about it?" Tanya asked.

"Some things. Have you heard about the theft at the Larimer Museum?"

Tanya squinted, the sign that she was thinking. "Yeah, I think I saw a post about it while I was scrolling through social media during my break."

"Well, that's my case. West Investigations provided the security for the exhibit."

Tanya sucked her teeth. "Not good."

"Definitely not good." He hesitated for a moment, but knew it was better that she heard it from him than stumble on the information somewhere else. "Maggie Scott is one of the curators at the Larimer. She's actually the curator responsible for the exhibit. She was hurt during the commission of the theft, not badly, but the police are also very suspicious of her at the moment."

"Kevin." Tanya closed her eyes and let her head fall to her chest.

"I know what you are going to say."

She opened one eye. "Do you?"

"Okay, what are you going to say?"

She lifted her head, both eyes open and pinned on him now. "I'm going to say that you should recuse yourself from this case. You and Maggie have a fraught history, and that is putting it mildly. I saw how torn up you were after you broke up with her. It took you years to get over her. This can come to no good for either of you."

"I wasn't torn up. I broke up with her."

Tanya snorted. "That may be, but you were broken-hearted." She held her hand up in a stop motion. "Save it. You threw yourself into football, but I know you. Heart. Broken."

"Whatever. That was a long time ago. We're both different people now."

"Yeah, that's why you haven't had a serious relationship since that relationship ended," his sister said pointedly.

"I've had relationships."

She rolled her eyes at him. "I said a serious relationship. One where you bring the woman home to meet Ma."

"This is a pointless conversation. This is my job. The other assistant curator, Maggie's friend, was found having apparently accidentally overdosed the same night as the theft, and Maggie insists on being involved in the investigation. There's nothing I can do."

Tanya set her now empty bowl aside. "Kevin, there's something you don't know."

He watched something flicker behind his sister's eyes. "What?"

She studied him for a long moment. He knew her well enough to see she was struggling with whatever it was she wanted to tell him.

He took her hands in his. "Hey, you know you can tell me anything, right? I'm your big bro. There are no secrets between us."

Tanya gave him a faint smile, slipping her hands from

his. "I know. I was just going to say that Maggie was really hurt when you left her."

His twin instinct told him that she was holding something back, but she spoke again before he could press her
on what it was.

"I don't say that to make you feel bad or guilty. It is
just a fact. I saw her a few times after you left, and she
was devastated. Just be careful. Be sure. I know you don't
want to hurt her again."

She unfolded from the sofa and carried her bowl into
the kitchen.

Be careful. Be sure.

He wasn't sure about anything at the moment except
that Maggie wouldn't hurt anyone, especially not someone she considered a friend. And she wouldn't be involved
in theft.

The Office's distinctive theme song began playing, the
credits rolling on the television screen, just as his cell
phone rang. He groaned when he saw Tess's name.

"What's up, Tess?"

"You need to get to the Larimer right away. We have
a problem."

IT FELT LIKE the situation had just taken a darker, more
sinister turn. Stealing a priceless ruby was one thing,
and they couldn't be sure yet if Kim's death was in any
way connected. But coming after Maggie now? When
the thief should be concerned about getting away with
the gem without getting caught, that meant they weren't
dealing with a run-of-the-mill criminal.

"Do you know anything about the curse that's mentioned in the note?" Francois had directed the question
to Maggie.

She looked shell-shocked, which made Kevin ache to wrap his arms around her. Tess eyed him. He kept his hands down by his sides.

The four of them stood in Maggie's office. After finding the letter, Maggie called Tess and the detective. She'd explained that Robert Gustev had held a staff meeting and kept her after for a brief discussion. He got the feeling that it hadn't been a positive discussion, but Francois didn't ask what it was about and Kevin hadn't wanted to step on the detective's toes. She'd found the envelope when she'd returned to her office.

Kevin assessed the space. It was neat and orderly. A handful of files were stacked on the corner of the desk, pens, a stapler and tape dispenser lined up in a row across the top edge. The books on the bookshelf behind the desk had been organized alphabetically by the author's last name. A printer sat on a credenza to the right of the door. There were no personal items at all. No photos of Maggie or a pet. No artwork on the wall, which he found surprising. But according to Maggie there was also nothing out of place or missing. Whoever had left the note had come in, dropped it on her desk and walked out. Their mystery person had likely touched nothing and spent less than twenty seconds inside the office.

Which meant there wouldn't be much to go on.

Maggie's voice pulled him out of his thoughts. "I have no idea what it means. I told you about the legend associated with the ruby, but I don't know anything about a curse."

Francois rubbed his chin. "Maybe the note writer meant the legend."

"The legend doesn't mention anything about people dying," Kevin pointed out.

"Yes, well…" Francois shrugged and slid the note into a plastic evidence bag.

Kevin could tell that Francois didn't think much of the threat, but it put him on edge. Even more on edge. Someone had come into Maggie's private space and lobbed a direct threat of violence. He couldn't just dismiss it as idle. The fact that there were no cameras in the areas only accessible by staff meant that any one of a number of people could have left the note, including someone who worked with Maggie.

Kevin had spent the last hour shadowing Francois while he'd questioned the staff members, but no one had admitted to seeing a stranger or anyone enter Maggie's office. He wasn't surprised by that. One thing he and Francois would probably agree on was that it seemed more and more likely that the person behind the theft, and now the threat against Maggie, was someone well known by Maggie and the employees of the Larimer. Someone who was pretty confident their presence in the areas of the museum restricted to employees wouldn't be notable if they were seen.

"I'll take the note in to be fingerprinted," Francois said.

"That's it?" Maggie shot back.

"There's not much more we can do, Ms. Scott. I'd urge the museum to increase its security measures. It wouldn't be a bad idea to install cameras in the employee work areas, at least the hallways here."

"Francois, this is a direct threat aimed at Maggie," Kevin said.

Francois darted a look between Kevin and Maggie, assessing.

Okay, so maybe he'd come on a bit too strong, but he didn't think the detective was taking this situation seriously enough. "And the LAPD is doing what it can to address the threat, but you know how these things go. Without more, my hands are tied." Francois looked at Maggie again. "Ms. Scott, you should remain vigilant about your surroundings. If you see or are approached by anyone suspicious, call me immediately." He handed Maggie his business card and shot a glance at Kevin. "Or I'm sure you can also call Mr. Lombard if you're feeling unsafe."

Kevin fought back the urge to punch the man.

"Kevin, a word please." Francois stepped out of Maggie's office and moved away down the hall where they wouldn't be overheard.

"Don't you think you might be getting too emotionally involved with this case?" Francois said, shooting a pointed glance at the door to Maggie's office.

"No, I don't." The lie hung between them. "Have you considered that your suspicion of Mag—Ms. Scott," Kevin corrected himself but not before Francois's brow cocked, "might be leading you to dismiss the danger she could be in?"

Francois scowled. "I'm not dismissing anything, including the possibility that Ms. Scott left this threatening letter for herself."

"Oh, come on." Francois was exasperating. "Why would she do that?"

"To take suspicion off herself." Francois held up a hand. "Look, I'll keep an open mind if you will. I think we can agree that whatever we're dealing, with Ms. Scott is at the center of it whether she wants to be or not."

"At the center, how?"

"Well, just look at the situation." Francois began ticking off his points using his fingers. "Ms. Scott advocated for bringing the ruby to the Larimer. She designed the exhibit and knew all about the security measures."

"She was one of several people who knew about the security measures for the Viperé."

"I'll give you that. She was at the museum the night the ruby was stolen."

"She was also attacked that night."

"True. She lives on the property where another museum employee was found dead, possibly murdered." Francois continued his list. "She was married to a man charged with embezzlement, who subsequently died, and no one can find the money. And now she has received a mysterious threat citing a curse no one seems to have heard of."

"None of that proves she had anything to do with the things that have happened."

Francois's scowl deepened. "I'm not a man who believes in coincidence. I'd think as a former law enforcement professional, you'd appreciate that."

"I think you're wrong about Maggie," Kevin said. "I think she's in real danger, and the reference in this threat to a curse might explain why."

"You think we might be dealing with some sort of conspiracy nut? A fanatic who's heard of or even made up some curse and associated it with the Viperé ruby?"

"I think it's possible. The internet can put all sorts of questionable ideas in people's heads, especially when there is already the hook of the so-called Viperé legends. I think it's definitely worth looking into."

Francois shook his head, but he was also rubbing his chin, a sign Kevin now knew that the detective was considering the point he'd made. "I have enough on my plate. I can't start chasing down curses. And—" he shot Kevin a pointed look "—I think you might be stretching here."

"Then I'll do it, but if I bring you something concrete, you have to promise you'll give it real consideration."

Francois considered for a moment longer before nodding. "Okay, but no cowboy stuff. If you find something, you bring it to me right away."

They shook on the deal.

Francois started to walk away then stopped and turned back. "Lombard, a word of advice. I know you think you can handle it, but it's very easy to lose your objectivity around a woman like Ms. Scott. I'd be careful if I were you."

Maggie was still standing exactly where she'd been when he'd left her office with Detective Francois. She looked scared and unsure. The urge to take her in his arms hit him again, even stronger this time.

"Come on. I'll take you home."

"Detective Francois thinks I left the note for myself, doesn't he? He thinks I was involved in the theft and that this is all just some big game I'm playing with everyone." Her voice was edging toward hysteria. "He probably thinks I killed Kim."

"Hey." Kevin reached out to her, and despite knowing what Detective Francois would say if he walked by and saw them, he pulled Maggie to his chest. "Francois is just doing his job. He'll come to see you had nothing to do with any of this."

Maggie pulled back just enough to look up at him with teary eyes. "You believe me though, don't you? You believe that I had nothing to do with any of this?"

He held her gaze. "I believe you."

Chapter Ten

I believe you.

Kevin's words bounced around in Maggie's mind during the drive from the Larimer to her house. She knew he'd been suspicious of her at first, but a good part of the weight, the fear, that she'd been carrying inside since she'd been attacked was alleviated by those three words.

I believe you.

She'd never developed such strong feelings so quickly for a man, but her attraction to Kevin was palpable and intense. She needed to keep it in check though. He seemed like a good investigator, as good a man as he was all those years ago, but it would be folly to trust him with her heart again.

He pulled to a stop in front of her cottage, and she exited the car, careful to avoid looking over at Kim's house. She didn't know how long she could keep living in the cottage, because of her feelings about Kim's death occurring only steps away and because she wasn't sure whether whatever relative of Kim's who inherited it would allow her to stay on the property. Just the idea of having to find a new place to live and move was too much to deal with, so she put the thought out of her mind. She just wanted to go inside and block out everything and everyone for a while.

She opened the door and turned back to Kevin. "Thank you for the ride."

"You're welcome. I'll be back in the morning to take you to work."

She jolted with surprise. "You don't have to do that."

"I know I don't have to, but in light of the assault against you and the threat today, I think it's best to err on the side of caution."

"I—"

She was cut off by the sound of her ringing phone. It was Apollo Bouras, the dealer she'd called earlier.

"It's one of the dealers I reached out to earlier today. I have to take this." She accepted the call.

Apollo was about twenty years older than Maggie, a Greek immigrant who knew everything there was to know about Southern European antiquities. He also did a fair amount of business as a go-between for sellers and buyers of rare gems.

"I'm sure you've heard about the theft of the Viperé ruby," Maggie said, jumping right into the heart of the call.

"Yes. Shocking," Apollo answered.

"Well, the museum is working with an investigator, and we'd like to pick your brain."

"Of course, of course. I will do anything I can to help you. You know that. Why don't you stop by the shop tomorrow? I'll be in all day as usual."

"Wonderful. Say tomorrow morning around nine thirty?" She looked at Kevin and got a nod from him confirming the time worked.

"Nine thirty is perfect," Apollo answered. "See you then."

She ended the call and turned back to Kevin.

"So I guess you will need that escort after all." The full-wattage smile he gave her sent her heart fluttering.

She returned the smile. "We could meet there." She was flirting, and it felt, well, it felt a little strange under the circumstances, but also exciting.

His gaze lowered to her mouth, and she noticed a subtle change in his expression. When his eyes met hers again there was a spark of desire there. The cool evening air warmed. She took a small step toward him, and he did the same, slipping his hand behind her head and lowering his mouth to hers.

The kiss was better than anything she had imagined, and she had to admit that she'd imagined kissing Kevin again several times over the years. She'd never forgotten what it felt like to be in his arms. The warm sensation quickly intensified into something fiery. She slid her hands up his chest and around his neck, pulling him closer and melding her body to his.

She'd forgotten how good a kisser he was. Extraordinary really. Need boiled inside of her. This couldn't be normal. The smoldering desire between them had to be some sort of response to the intensity of the situation they found themselves in.

She pulled back from the kiss. "I should go in."

He stepped back, his eyes shrouded. "I'll pick you up in the morning."

"Good night, Kevin."

His dark brown eyes were piercing. "Sleep tight, Maggie."

MAGGIE SPENT A fitful night tossing and turning. The few snatches of sleep she was able to get alternated between grief-riddled dreams of Kim and memories of her past relationship with Kevin. Her past and present were colliding in an emotional tumult that felt like it had the potential to spin out of control. She awoke more exhausted than she'd been when she fell asleep.

She was working on her second mug of coffee when Kevin rang her doorbell, and she let him in.

He held out the to-go cup in his hand. "Looks like you don't need this," he said, handing her the cup.

She smiled and took the cup. "Not right now, but probably later."

He cocked his head to the side. "Didn't get much sleep last night?"

Heat crept up her neck as she recalled the dreams she'd had about him. "Not much, no." She turned away from him, carrying her empty coffee mug to the sink. "We should get going."

Even with her back to him, she could feel Kevin's frown. After a moment, he rose and tossed his trash in the garbage bin.

She grabbed her purse from the sofa as they passed through the living room and headed for the front door.

A police cruiser and an unmarked black sedan pulled into the driveway as she locked up.

Detective Francois stepped out of the sedan and walked toward her and Kevin. He stopped at the bottom of her stoop.

"Ms. Scott." He held a piece of paper out to her. "I have a warrant to search these premises."

As a former police officer, Kevin was used to search warrants, but he wasn't usually on this side of the execution.

"Can I see that?" He gestured to the warrant in Maggie's shaking hand. She was looking at it, but he could tell she wasn't seeing the words. She handed him the papers.

He skimmed them, looking for the most important piece of information. The suspected crime that Francois listed to justify the search. Felony theft. Second-degree murder.

Murder.

That must mean the police had determined that Kim Sumika hadn't accidentally overdosed.

He skimmed the rest of the warrant, noting the items the officers were allowed to seize. It was pretty typical. Electronics. Diaries. Writings. Receipts. Medications. Disposable gloves. Cleaning products. Vacuums. The warrant also gave Francois the right to search Maggie's car and phone.

So Francois thought Maggie could have killed her best friend, cleaned up after herself then pulled off the theft of a priceless ruby.

He caught Francois's eyes, but the man was good. He saw nothing there.

"I don't understand. I didn't do anything," Maggie pleaded.

Francois turned to her. "Ms. Scott, I understand this has to be upsetting for you. You are welcome to stay as long as you do nothing to interfere with the search in any way. We should only be an hour or two since your residence isn't terribly large."

"Should I have a lawyer present?" Maggie's gaze darted to him.

The knot in his stomach grew. He wished he could do or say something to help her in that instant, but he knew there was nothing. Francois had a warrant, and that gave him the power to be there. They could only make the situation worse. "You could," he started to say.

"But we do not have to wait for your attorney to arrive before beginning our search," Francois declared, correctly.

Kevin worked to check the anger he felt toward the detective at the moment. "Detective Francois, could I speak with you for a moment. Please," he added when the detective looked ready to refuse.

Francois hesitated for a moment then nodded.

They walked to the end of the driveway, away from the two officers who had shown up with Francois.

"It's not personal," Francois said. "I'm just doing my job. Maggie Scott had the means and opportunity to carry out the theft of the ruby and the murder of Kim Sumika."

"Let's slow down for a minute. You know for sure Kim Sumika's death was a homicide?"

Francois looked as if he was kicking himself for having said too much. He pressed his lips together tightly.

"Francois. Detective, please. I would really appreciate it if you could tell me what you can."

Francois sighed heavily. "The coroner found heroin and Rohypnol in Kim Sumika's system. The killer may have thought we wouldn't check, but Dr. Brown is thorough."

"So the killer sedates Kim with the Rohypnol then injects her with the heroin, making it look like she overdosed."

"That's the working theory at the moment."

"You still have a timing issue. Maggie was at the museum when Kim Sumika was killed."

"Sumika's house is only ten minutes from the museum. That gives Maggie plenty of time to get to Kim's place, slip her the overdose and get back to the museum in time to be 'assaulted'—" Francois made air quotes "—giving her a pretty good alibi for the theft and murder."

"Come on!" Kevin shook his head, accentuating the absurdity of the idea.

"You know how this goes, Lombard. If she's innocent, we'll find nothing and move on, but you know I have to do this."

He understood where Francois was coming from. He'd stood in his exact spot hundreds of times and not that long ago. That didn't mean he liked it now.

"I'm going to take Maggie out of here."

"That's fine. You'll have to take your car though. We'll need hers for searching and processing. It's included in the warrant. And, Ms. Scott, we'll need your phone before you leave. If you give me a minute, I can have a tech copy the hard drive now, and I can give it right back."

Kevin appreciated the gesture.

He started back toward Maggie, but Francois's hand on his arm stopped him.

"Lombard, I am keeping an open mind here, I assure you," Francois said with a seriousness that hardened his jaw. His gaze darted to Maggie then back to Kevin's face. "You would do well to do the same."

Chapter Eleven

The sky was cloudless, the day already warm even though it was only midmorning. Maggie stared out of the car window as Kevin drove. They stopped at a red light, and she watched a group of kids, about middle school age, amble down the sidewalk, chatting and laughing, backpacks strapped to their backs. It was a picture-perfect day, and yet Maggie felt like she was in purgatory. She hadn't understood most of what was written in the search warrant, but several words had stood out.

Theft.

Second-degree murder.

Detective Francois thought she'd killed Kim.

She was a murder suspect.

Despite her question about having a lawyer present at the search, the reality was she didn't have the money for a lawyer. She was barely getting by. If not for Kim offering her a cut-rate rent far below the going market, she wouldn't have been able to afford to live in such a nice neighborhood so close to the Larimer.

A lump grew in her throat, but she was determined not to cry. He'd suggested they head out to meet with her dealer friend as they'd planned, and she'd agreed. The last thing she wanted to do was stand around while strangers pawed through her belongings.

Her phone dinged, indicating she'd received a text message. Her father had made a 1:15 p.m. lunch reservation at a restaurant she wasn't familiar with in Chinatown.

She couldn't hold back the groan that escaped as she read it.

"What is it? Is everything okay?" Kevin darted a look at her from the driver's side of the car.

"No, but yes. Nothing for you to worry about. It's just my father."

Kevin grinned. "How is Boyd?"

"Getting married."

Kevin's grin widened. "I guess he's pretty good then."

She groaned. "He wants me to meet his fiancée today over lunch. What kind of woman willingly becomes a man's seventh wife? The man is clearly incapable of making a real commitment to anyone."

"I know Boyd was a nontraditional father, but he's a good guy. A bit impulsive, but he embraces life."

"Of course you'd take his side. He always liked you, probably because he saw so much of himself in you."

A heavy silence fell over the car.

"I'm sorry. I shouldn't have said that."

"You don't have to be sorry for how you feel. I hurt you. From your perspective, I can see how you view me and your father as alike. But, Maggie, I was a twenty-year-old idiot when I walked away from you. I didn't realize what I had until it was too late. And I was even stupider for not crawling back to you on my hands and knees once I realized what a fool I'd been. But I want a second chance."

"Kevin, I can't do this right now."

"No, I know. It's terrible timing, but let me do one thing. Let me go to lunch with you."

She was surprised. "You want to be my date to lunch to meet my father's fiancée?"

"Yes, you said it yourself, your dad and I get along well. I can help keep the conversation going, smooth over any awkward bumps and be a sounding board for your inevitable meltdown afterward."

She slid a sidelong glance at him. "I'm not going to melt down."

"Of course you won't. So what do you say?"

It wasn't a bad idea. He could be a buffer if she needed one.

"Okay." She hesitated. "But about this second chance."

He reached for her hand. "I meant it. I'm not going to run away this time. I know that I want a second chance with you. You may not want the same, and I'll have to live with that if you don't, but I'm putting it out there. Just think about it, okay?"

She nodded. It was going to be hard not to think about it, but there was a more pressing situation facing them at the moment. She forced herself to focus on it.

Kevin parked in the lot behind the store, and they made their way to Xanthe's Treasures. The chime from the security system rang out as they stepped through the doors.

Antiques filled every shelf and cabinet, and Maggie knew each item had been carefully curated by Apollo Bouras. The items that were worth substantial amounts were locked in glass cases strategically placed in the space.

Apollo flashed a quick smile as she and Kevin entered, before turning back to the customer he'd been working with, an older woman who reeked of money in a black-and-white-checked Chanel suit, string pearls and low-heeled pumps.

They milled around the store while Apollo finished with his client.

It took close to fifteen minutes for Apollo's customer to finally settle on her purchases and pay. Apollo kept a cheery smile on his face until the woman had left the store and disappeared from sight.

"Finally. Mrs. Lowell is richer than a sultan, but the woman is just so indecisive."

"It's fine. We didn't have a problem waiting." She exchanged air kisses with Apollo.

"Maggie, my God! How could something like this have happened?" Apollo said, holding her at arm's length. "I can't believe it."

"Me either, but I'm hoping you can help. Oh, excuse my rudeness. This is Kevin Lombard. His firm has been hired by the board of directors of the museum to try and locate the Viperé ruby."

The two men shook hands.

Apollo focused on Maggie again, confusion wrinkling his brow. "And you're here because of the Viperé?"

"Well, we think it's possible the thief has plans to sell the Viperé on the black market."

Apollo looked thoughtful. "That would make some sense. It's quite valuable. Even more so if the thief is able to find someone who will cut it for him."

Maggie brought a hand to her throat, a small gasp escaping.

Apollo chuckled. "Don't stroke out on me. It's just speculation."

"I honestly hadn't thought about the thief cutting the ruby," she answered.

"Why would it be more valuable cut?" Kevin asked.

"It would be easier to conceal and move for one thing.

The authorities are on the lookout for a large ruby, not several small rubies," Maggie answered.

"And the thief could likely get more money overall as long as he finds someone who knows what they are doing when they cut the stone. It's like those investors who buy a company, chop it up and sell it for parts. Sometimes the parts are worth more than the whole. In this case, smaller stones can be set in several different settings, obscuring the origin of the whole."

Kevin nodded his head in understanding, but Maggie was still dealing with the shock of realizing the Viperé stone might not even exist any longer. At least, not in its original form.

"We're actually here looking for your help," Kevin said, giving her a look.

"Yes." She shook the shock away. Until she knew otherwise, she was going to assume the ruby was intact. And pray it stayed that way. "I know you have handled transactions involving jewelry and gems of a certain significance. Have you or any other dealer you know of had an inquiry from someone asking about the Viperé ruby?"

Apollo looked uncomfortable. "You know I keep my clients' information in the strictest of confidences."

Kevin's mouth tightened. "We could have the police visit."

Apollo frowned.

Maggie placed a hand on his forearm. Apollo required honey, not vinegar. "Apollo, I know you have the utmost integrity. We're not asking for confidential information. Just whether there's been anyone asking about the Viperé."

Apollo still did not look happy. "No. Not asking about the Viperé."

"But someone was asking about rubies?" she pressed.

"Not rubies per se, but whether I knew about any large, precious gemstones that might be on the market, or coming onto the market soon. I didn't have, or know of, a current seller, so I couldn't help the potential buyer."

"And who was this potential buyer?" Kevin said.

Apollo hesitated again.

"Please, Apollo," Maggie said.

Apollo gave a resigned sigh. "I can't imagine he'd have anything to do with the theft anyway. The Larimer is his museum, after all."

Maggie felt herself leaning in. "His museum?"

Apollo nodded. "Carter Tutwilder. He's the potential buyer who made the inquiry."

CARTER TUTWILDER'S OFFICE was in Los Angeles's financial district. Maggie called ahead to Tutwilder Industries, explaining who she was and that she'd like to speak to Mr. Tutwilder at his earliest convenience, that day if it was at all possible. Tutwilder had agreed to give them ten minutes.

The Tutwilder family had a long and storied history on the West Coast and in the Midwest. The family had built their fortune in agribusiness. They had their hands in farming, fuel, fisheries, grain and other commodities, as well as biotechnology, to name just a few industries that had contributed to their multibillion dollar fortune. Still, the family somehow managed to remain under the radar and out of the public eye.

Kevin pulled into a garage two blocks from the Wilshire Grand Center, and he and Maggie walked to the building.

Office space in the Wilshire went for thousands of dollars per square foot, and Kevin had no doubt that Tutwilder's offices would be among the grandest. He wasn't disappointed. Tutwilder Industries' offices comprised floors twenty-five through twenty-nine.

He and Maggie signed in with security in the lobby then took the elevator to the twenty-ninth floor.

The office suite was decorated in rich, dark colors of walnut and burgundy that gave the space an elegant and expensive feel.

An attractive young brunette looked up from her computer monitor as they made their way to her desk.

"Good afternoon and welcome to Tutwilder Industries. How may I help you today?" She smiled.

"We have an appointment with Mr. Tutwilder," Maggie said.

"And your names?"

Maggie gave their names, and the receptionist clicked a few keys on the computer. "Yes, of course. One moment, please."

The receptionist reached for the phone. She spoke softly into the receiver before hanging up and standing.

"Mr. Tutwilder is ready for you now. If you'll follow me, please."

Kevin looked at Maggie with raised eyebrows. He hadn't expected it to be so easy to get in to see a man like Tutwilder, but he'd been impressed when Maggie had convincingly argued to whichever gatekeeper she'd spoken to about arranging this meeting that Mr. Tutwilder would want to do whatever he could to help them find the Viperé ruby. And from all appearances, it had worked.

The receptionist led them down a long corridor full of large offices and busy-looking people in them. They stopped at the only office with a frosted-glass door and no nameplate.

The receptionist rapped on the door and waited until a brisk "come in" came from the other side.

She pushed open the door, and he and Maggie stepped around her and inside a spacious office outfitted with buttery black leather furniture and a massive glass-topped desk. But the showstopper was the view. A glass wall of windows overlooked downtown Los Angeles.

Carter Tutwilder rose from behind his desk.

"Ms. Scott," he said, circling the desk and offering his hand. "And you must be Kevin Lombard. Tess Stenning had said wonderful things about you. I trust you are getting close to finding the criminals who have absconded with the Viperé ruby."

"I am doing everything in my power along with the police," he said, shaking the man's hand.

The receptionist slipped from the room, shutting the door behind her.

Tutwilder made his way back behind the desk, and Kevin took the opportunity to really study the man.

He had the presence and confidence of someone who'd been born into wealth and privilege. He stood tall in a black suit that looked like it had been made specifically for him, which it probably had. The tailoring was impeccable, but it didn't quite mask the soft upper body. His face showed the beginnings of a double chin, and his hair had been combed over to hide a bald spot at his crown, again expertly, but there was only so much that could be done to fight a receding hairline.

Tutwilder sat, waving them into the chairs across from his desk. "So, how can I help you?"

"You are the chairman of the board of the Larimer Museum," Kevin started them off.

"Correct. And one of the museum's largest donors."

Maggie smiled. "You and the members of your family are very generous, and the museum appreciates it more than I can say."

Tutwilder relaxed, leaning back in his chair. "I'm happy to do it. The arts are so important and artists so under-appreciated by society. There never seems to be enough funding."

"As one of the biggest donors, you received an invitation to the open house two nights ago, correct?"

Tutwilder smiled, but it wasn't as bright as the smile he'd given them when they'd entered. "I see where you're going with this. I did receive an invitation to the opening, of course, but unfortunately I had a prior commitment and could not make it."

"But you have an extensive art collection—" Kevin paused with intention "—that includes a collection of rare gems, I understand."

Tutwilder's eyes narrowed. "I do, although it's not common knowledge. I'd sure like to know how you came across that information."

He returned Tutwilder's narrow gaze. "I am an investigator."

"A very good one it would seem," Tutwilder said in a clipped tone.

"Mr. Tutwilder—"

"Ah, now, Ms. Scott. Please call me Carter."

"And I'm Maggie. Carter, please know that we mean no offense. Kevin and I thought that with your knowledge of gems you might be able to help point us in a few directions that we might not otherwise think of."

Kevin studied Tutwilder and saw that he wasn't buying Maggie's buttering him up. You didn't run a multibillion dollar corporation and not develop well-honed instincts for when someone was attempting to pull one over on you. He'd conducted enough suspect interviews to know that the best way to get information out of Tutwilder would be to go directly at him. He'd definitely anger the man, but it would be that anger that tripped him up.

"Where do you keep your collections?"

"That is need-to-know information, Mr. Lombard."

"I'm sure the LAPD will feel they need to know. I can call Detective Francois."

"Carter—" Maggie started then stopped abruptly when Tutwilder held up a hand.

"What are you suggesting? That I had something to do with the theft of the Viperé ruby?"

"I'm not suggesting anything," Kevin shot back. "I'm asking questions and seeking answers."

"Well, I don't like your questions."

"And I don't like your answers. We have it on good authority that you were asking about the purchase of rare jewels just a few weeks ago."

"We?" Tutwilder's angry gaze slid to Maggie's face.

Maggie wrapped her hand around his forearm and squeezed. "Carter—" she tried again.

And again Tutwilder cut her off. "I don't know where you are getting your information, but it appears you aren't as good an investigator as I first thought."

"So you haven't been looking to acquire more jewels for your private collection?"

"Mr. Lombard, what I am or am not looking to acquire is none of your concern." Tutwilder looked at Maggie. "Or yours, Ms. Scott. Now, I squeezed you into my schedule because I thought I might be of some help. I can see that I was mistaken. I really don't have any more time for you today."

Tutwilder slid on the glasses lying on his desk, an obvious dismissal.

Maggie gripped his arm tighter, goading him to stand.

Tutwilder could kick them out of his office, but he couldn't stop them from looking for more information on his collection.

"What the hell were you thinking?" Maggie whirled on him the moment they stepped into the elevator. "That man is my boss's boss, kind of. He's basically the head of the museum, and I'm already on thin ice. I can't afford to lose my job."

He didn't break eye contact. "Your job is the last thing you should be worried about right now. You could be on the verge of losing your freedom if we don't give Detective Francois someone else to focus on quickly."

Maggie stalled hard then focused on the closed elevator doors.

He sighed internally. This had not gone the way he'd hoped. "Look, I'm sorry if I came on strong in there, but Carter Tutwilder is lying."

Maggie didn't answer. They made the walk back to the car silently. She didn't speak until he'd paid the parking fee and they were headed out of the garage. "Even if he is lying, how are we going to prove it?"

His stomach churned because that was the million-dollar question and one he didn't have an answer to. "I don't know, but I will."

Chapter Twelve

Maggie would have liked to continue pushing ahead on the case, but it was 12:40 p.m. They were meeting her father and his fiancée at 1:15 p.m. Of course, when it came to her father, 1:15 p.m. more likely meant 1:30 p.m. or even 2:00 p.m., but she didn't want to be the one who was late to the party, so to speak.

"Do you need to stop by the museum before we head to the restaurant?" Kevin asked.

"No. There's no time and no point."

She really should call Robert and let him know she wouldn't be in until later in the afternoon. They didn't punch timecards at the museum. There were times when they were expected to stay late or come in early, so everyone just kept their own schedule. It wasn't unusual for any of them to take a half day for personal reasons, so it shouldn't be a problem that she hadn't gotten to work yet. *Shouldn't*, though, was the operative word. It still hurt that Robert had tried to sideline her. She skipped the call and shot Robert a text telling him she'd be in after lunch.

The restaurant was in Chinatown.

She and Kevin were the first to arrive, but they were seated immediately. The hostess had just walked away from the table when the door to the restaurant opened and Boyd Scott entered.

Her father and a woman who could only be Julie walked into the restaurant holding hands, and Maggie was instantly thankful that Kevin had invited himself to come along.

The panic must have shown on her face because Kevin leaned over from where he sat by her side and said, "You doing okay?"

She couldn't form words at the moment, but she smiled and nodded.

Just be polite and keep it together for one lunch. That was all she had to do. That wasn't hard. She was an adult, after all.

"Maggie," her father said, coming to a stop beside the table. He wore a sports jacket and khaki pants. The dark brown skin on the top of his head hadn't seen hair for more than two decades, but he still wore a neatly trimmed mustache above his top lip.

Maggie stood and let him pull her into a bear hug. He smelled as he usually did, like cigars. The familiarity of it put her more at ease. This was her father, Boyd, a new woman on his arm, but he was the same as always.

"This," her father said, reaching behind him for the hand of the woman he'd come into the restaurant with, "is Julie." He pulled Julie to his side.

Julie wore a ruffled white shirt, a peasant skirt with colorful flowers all over it and gold goddess sandals that laced up her legs. Her makeup was as colorful as her outfit—bursts of pink on her lips, her eyelids and her cheeks. Her blond hair was streaked with gray and piled atop her head in a messy updo. The thing that surprised Maggie most though was her age. Her father's girlfriends had trended down in age for the last decade and a half. Based on that, Maggie had been expecting a woman in her mid to early thirties. She had to be at least a decade older than thirty, which still made her more than a decade younger than her father, but at least she wasn't younger than Maggie like the last woman her father had insisted she meet. She knew it wasn't forward-thinking or liberated to care about the age difference between two consenting adults, and usually she didn't, but this was her father. Maybe it was childish and immature, but it was weird to think about her father dating someone younger than she was.

A wave of sickly sweet perfume came at Maggie as Julie threw her arms around her. "It's so nice to finally meet you."

"Oh! It's, ah, it's nice to meet you too."

"I'm sorry," Julie said, taking two steps back. "I'm a hugger. Especially when I'm nervous. I just want us to get along."

"Honey, now don't you worry about that. I know you and Maggie are going to get along swimmingly. Just you wait and see. Kevin!"

Several heads at the tables around them turned. Boyd Scott was a man with a personality that grabbed attention even when he didn't mean to.

Kevin stood. "Mr. Scott." Kevin extended a hand.

Body shook it heartily. "It's been a long time. I'm glad to see you and Maggie are spending time together again. Maybe you two will finally get your acts together then."

"Dad."

"Boyd, darling. Let's sit," Julie said, seeming to catch on quicker than her fiancé to Maggie's distress at his comments. "We have all lunch to catch up with the kids."

Maggie frowned. Now she was one of the kids. This woman barely knew her.

Kevin squeezed her hand. "You can do this," he mouthed.

She sucked in a deep breath and let it out slowly as they settled in at the table.

Maggie reached for the wine list. There was no way she was getting through this lunch without liquid help.

"Let's have champagne," her father said. "After all, we are celebrating. And it's on me."

Maggie's eyebrows arched. The restaurant her father had chosen wasn't going to be getting any spreads in a magazine, but it wasn't cheap either.

Her father laughed. "I know. I know. But I got a job."

Maggie's brow climbed higher.

"I didn't want to tell you until I got through the probationary period, but I've been working for a nonprofit for older adults. The organization provides classes—computer, horticultural, painting—and social activities like dances and cocktail hours. It's like summer camp for us mature individuals, but since most of the people who sign up are retired, we can do it all year round."

Maggie set the wine list down. "Wow, Dad, that's great. Congratulations."

Her father beamed. "Thank you, baby. That's actually how Julie and I met. She teaches the gardening and horticulture classes at the center."

"My husband and I used to own our own landscaping business," Julie added.

"Oh, that's great." What she knew about gardening could fit on a Post-it. She didn't even have plants in her house, couldn't keep them alive. But if Julie had owned a business, she wasn't under the illusion that marrying her father would be some sort of financial windfall.

"I started going to the center to have something to fill my days with," Boyd continued telling the story of how he and Julie met, "and when the office assistant moved to Phoenix to be with her children, the manager offered me the job."

Their waiter arrived. Her father ordered champagne for the table, and they each placed their orders. The restaurant had pretty standard American fare. Her father and Kevin ordered burgers and fries, Julie got the salmon and Maggie ordered the chicken salad.

"So, how long have you two been dating?" Kevin asked once the waiter had hurried off the put in their orders.

Boyd's brow arched. "I could ask the same question of you two."

"We're not dating, Dad."

"No? Then what is he doing here? No offense there, Kevin, but it's been a minute since I've seen you and my daughter together. Always liked you, though. I figured when you disappeared and Maggie stopped talking about you that she'd thrown you back into the ocean, so to speak."

"We're friends, Dad. I thought we were here to get to know Julie," she said, attempting to divert her father's attention from her love life to his own.

Kevin's shoulders shook with suppressed laughter.

"We are, we are. I want my two favorite ladies in the whole wide world to get to love each other as much as I love you both. But—" her father held his hand out palm up "—you can't just show up with your long-lost first love and expect me not to ask questions. I am your father."

Maggie massaged her temples.

"Boyd, darling, I think you're embarrassing Maggie.

She is your daughter, but she's a grown woman who may not want to talk about her love life with her father."

Maggie shot Julie a look of gratitude. Maybe she wasn't so terrible.

"So, Julie, why horticulture?" Kevin said, finally doing what she'd brought him along to do—keep the situation from going off the rails.

Julie explained that her husband had started the business before they'd met, and after they married she'd joined him. He'd passed away from a heart attack four years earlier. Their three children were scattered across the country, and none of them had the green thumb their parents had, so she'd sold the company after her husband's death.

The waiter came back with the champagne as she'd talked, and they toasted to the engagement.

Maggie had to admit, Julie wasn't what she'd expected and her father seemed genuinely happy. Not that he hadn't seemed happy at the beginning of the relationships with his other wives, but he did seem different with Julie. More grounded. The woman was an expert at rooting things. Maybe she'd found a way to give her father roots.

They ate and chatted, and Maggie found herself genuinely liking Julie. In addition to her job at the center, Julie liked to sew and paint and to visit with her grandchildren. Maggie was reeling a bit from the realization that once her father and Julie married, she'd have stepsiblings. At the age of thirty-six, she was finally going to have a sister and two brothers. And five step nieces and nephews. As much as she'd always wished she'd had more family, it was all suddenly a bit much to take in.

More than anything, she was thankful that the theft at the museum didn't come up. She was not surprised her father didn't know about the theft or Kim's death. He wasn't much of a paper reader and didn't particularly care for art. She didn't want to worry him nor did she want to hash through the mess that was her life at the moment.

Her head spun, and she felt sick to her stomach. She pushed her chair back from the table abruptly. "Excuse me for a moment."

She rose and made her way toward the restrooms.

"Maggie." Julie rushed to catch up to her at the door to the ladies' room. "Your father wanted me to check on you and make sure you were okay."

"I'm fine." She tried for a smile. "I think I might have had a little too much champagne."

Julie laid a light hand on Maggie's forearm. "I just wanted to let you know that I love your father and I plan to do my very best to make him happy. And I hope that we can forge our own relationship."

Maggie didn't have to force a smile this time. "I hope so too."

Maggie's phone rang.

"I should be getting back to the table. I'm sure the guys are eager to know you're okay."

The call was from Robert. "I'll be there in a moment. This is my boss. Probably wanting to know when I'm coming in today."

Maggie accepted the call as Julie made her way back to the table.

"Hi, Robert. I know I should have called you and let you know that I was going to be in late today, but this morning has been hectic."

"That's one way to put it. I just got off the phone with Carter Tutwilder."

Crap.

"I know I should have called you first—"

"It wouldn't have made a difference. Carter was not pleased to hear that the police searched your home this morning."

"How did Carter even know about that?"

"Are you saying it's not true?" Robert shot back.

"No. The police did search my home this morning, but I had nothing to do with that. They are investigating—"

"Yes, they are. And in order for them to have gotten a search warrant for your home, they'd have to have some sort of evidence that you could be involved in a crime. I'm sorry, Maggie, we just can't have that kind of rumor and supposition associated with the Larimer."

Her jaw clenched. "Robert, we've discussed this."

"That was before. Carter and the board agree. Until this matter is resolved, you are being placed on administrative leave."

She was sure Carter had agreed. She didn't know how he found out about the search of her house, but she had no doubt that his decision to have the board put her on administrative leave was motivated by the meeting they'd just had.

"Until the matter is over. Robert, police investigations can take months. Even years."

Administrative leave meant no paycheck. They may as well have fired her. They probably would. They just wanted to get their ducks in a row before they did.

"I'm sorry, Maggie. I'll have the personal effects from your office shipped to your house."

The line went dead.

"Maggie?"

She turned to find Kevin behind her.

"You okay?" he asked, concern crinkling the skin around his eyes.

She shook her head. "No, no, I'm not." It was happening again. Losing her job. Being suspected of having committed a crime. Being ostracized. Just like it had in New York with Ellison.

She swallowed and said the words that sent panic streaking through her. "I just got fired."

Chapter Thirteen

Maggie went back to the table and pleaded sickness to her father and Julie, promising that they'd get together again soon. Now she and Kevin stood outside in front of the restaurant.

She turned angry eyes on him. "I just lost my job. The board has voted to put me on administrative leave until the police case is over." The words burned their way out of her throat.

"I'm sorry. I—" Kevin reached out to her, but she stepped back, away from his touch.

"You went into Tutwilder's office like a bull in a china shop and basically accused the chairman of the board of the museum of what? Stealing a priceless artifact." She shook with anger.

Kevin held his hands out. "Look, I could have been more diplomatic. I wasn't thinking."

"That's just it. You never think about me. When we were together in college, it was all about you."

Kevin's face hardened. "It was never about me. It was about making money so my mom didn't have to struggle anymore and so Tanya wouldn't have to worry about paying for medical school."

"Was it?" she shot back at him. "That's why you played

football. Why you went into the NFL. But it doesn't explain why you dumped me." Her voice dropped low. "We were planning a life together after graduation. A family. And then, just like that—" she snapped her fingers "—you were out. Gone." She looked at him and all the hurt she'd felt the moment he told her it was over welled up again. "And what? Now you want a second chance?"

"Walking away from you was the biggest mistake of my life. I have and will always regret it and I am more sorry than I can ever express. I know I hurt you—"

"You have no idea," she hissed. Hot tears rolled down her cheeks. She wished she could stop them, but she was well past controlling her emotions. Or the words that were tumbling from her mouth. "I was pregnant."

Kevin stilled, the color fleeing from his face.

"I found out a week after you broke up with me," she continued. "And the next week, I miscarried."

"You were pregnant?" His voice was barely audible. "Why didn't you tell me?"

"Because you weren't there." The accusation whipped from her lips.

He flinched.

"And then it didn't matter."

Anger flashed in his eyes. "It mattered. You should have told me."

"No." She pointed at him. "I was nineteen, pregnant, and the man I thought was going to love me forever had just walked out on me. You of all people do not get to judge my choices."

His jaw clenched. "I had a right to know."

She stepped forward, holding his gaze. "Then you should have been there."

A long moment passed.

"Is that why you married Ellison after we broke up? Because I wasn't there?"

She shook her head, some of the anger she felt toward him dissipating. It was useless being angry. It wouldn't get her job back, and it wouldn't change anything. "I'm not doing this with you. The past is in the past, and that's where I'm leaving it."

She turned and started away from him.

"Where are you going?" He jogged to catch up with her.

"Home." She pulled out her phone and called up the rideshare app. "I'll get there myself."

"Maggie—"

"No." She turned to him, looking him in the eye. "I don't want to be around you right now, Kevin."

KEVIN CAUGHT TANYA at her apartment the next morning before she left for her shift at the hospital. Tanya already had her coat on, thermos of hot coffee in hand, when she opened the door to him.

"Kevin? Hi, what's up? Are you okay?" she asked, stepping back so he could enter the apartment.

He didn't waste time or mince words. "You knew about Maggie's miscarriage? About the baby, didn't you?"

"How did you—"

"Maggie told me. That's what you were going to tell me the other day before you stopped yourself."

Tanya sighed and set her thermos down on the side table next to her purse. "I knew."

"Why didn't you tell me?" Fury rose in his tone.

"Because I couldn't. Maggie came into the student health center once she realized she might be pregnant. You know I held a work-study job there while we were

in school. I was on duty. Patient confidentiality laws pro-
hibited me from saying anything to you or anyone about
a patient's medical history."

He glowered at her. "You're my sister. It's been years."

She shook her head. "It doesn't matter who I am or how
many years it's been. Confidentiality still applies. And,
to be honest with you, I'm not sure I would have told you
if I could have."

He threw up his hands. "Is everybody losing their
minds?" he yelled.

"Kevin, there was nothing you could have done. Mis-
carriages are common, much more common than most
people even realize. Telling you would have only left you
feeling guilty for something that you had no control over."
She reached out, placing a hand on his arm. "Something
that was not in any way your fault, do you understand me?"

He understood her just like she understood where his
anger emanated from. Fear. Fear that his decision to break
up with Maggie had upset her enough to cause a miscarriage.

"If I hadn't left—" he said softly.

"She would have still lost the baby," Tanya said firmly.

"I should have been there for her."

"What is it Mom always says, 'the shoulda, woulda,
couldas will drive you up a wall if you let them'?" She
gave him a small smile. "You can't change the choices you
made, and you shouldn't want to. Right or wrong, they
made you, and to some extent Maggie, who you are now.
And you're not that bad." She gave a little sister shrug he
knew was intended to draw a smile from him.

He wasn't ready to smile, but talking to his sister did
make him feel a little better. It didn't alleviate all his guilt.
He wasn't sure anything could do that, but he felt a little

lighter than he had when he'd walked into her apartment. He pulled his sister into a tight hug.

"So Maggie finally told you," Tanya said after they pulled apart. "Interesting."

"What's interesting about it? She was mad at me for getting her fired, and she shot it at me like a bullet."

Tanya's mouth fell open. "You got her fired?"

He ran a hand over his head. His life felt as if it was spinning out of control, and he didn't like it. "Not on purpose. I came on a little strong when questioning her boss's boss, and he's taking it out on her."

"You remember what I said about you. Maggie. This case." She threw her hands up in a gesture simulating an explosion. "Kaboom."

"I know, I—"

"Should have listened to your younger, but wiser, sister." She pressed her palms to her chest. "Yes, you should have."

"Didn't you just say something about 'shoulda, woulda, couldas'? I'm trying to remember what that was."

"Point taken. So what are you going to do now?"

"I have to get my head on straight and focus. West Investigations has been hired to find the ruby, and I'm convinced its theft is somehow tied to Maggie's friend's murder."

"And Maggie is intent on helping solve said friend's murder." Tanya looped her purse over her shoulder and picked up her thermos. "Well, maybe you'll have the rarest of opportunities, big brother. You might be able to rectify some of your 'shoulda, woulda, couldas.'"

Chapter Fourteen

"Thanks for coming in," Detective Francois said, settling into the chair on the opposite side of the table from Maggie.

Maggie had spent the first morning of her forced leave giving her house a deep clean and chastising herself for letting her anger get the better of her the day before with Kevin. Detective Francois had shown up on her doorstep around noon, requesting her presence down at the station for a formal interview. He'd posed it as a question, but she'd gotten the distinct impression she didn't have a choice.

She'd hesitated a moment, wondering if she should have a lawyer present, but had dismissed the idea quickly. She had nothing to hide. The faster Detective Francois saw that she'd had nothing to do with the theft or Kim's murder, the quicker he could turn his attention to viable suspects.

So she'd ridden to the police station beside him in his unmarked police sedan.

He'd shown her into an interrogation room and offered her coffee and water, which she'd declined. She considered a lawyer a second time when Detective Francois read her Miranda rights, but she again rejected the idea. She didn't have the money, and she didn't have anything to hide.

"There are just a few things I want to clarify." He looked up from the notepad in front of him and gave her a smile she guessed was meant to be disarming. To her, it looked a little more predatory. No matter how polite Detective Francois was, she wasn't going to make the mistake of thinking that he was her friend. He was looking for a thief and a murderer, and right now she knew she was his best suspect.

She flashed him a quick smile. "Anything I can do to help, Detective. Have you made any headway with Kim's case?"

His smile tightened. "I assure you we are doing everything we can."

"I'm sure you are," she lied.

"Just so I'm sure I have things correct, can you go over the night of the theft and finding Ms. Sumika's body again?"

Maggie bit back her frustration and walked the detective through the worst night of her life once again.

"And when was the last time, before you found Ms. Sumika, that you were in her house?"

Maggie thought for a moment. "Two evenings before. Kim invited me over for dinner. She did that on occasion. She did seem a little distracted."

Detective Francois perked up. "Distracted? How?"

"Like she had something on her mind. I asked her about it, and she said it was nothing." Guilt hung heavy on her heart. "I wish I'd pressed her on it."

"You have no idea what might have been worrying her?"

"No. I was assigned to take the lead on designing the Viperé exhibit, but we were all under a bit of stress with the donors' open house coming up and making sure everything went as scheduled. I remember thinking that it could just be that."

"Huh." He wrote something she couldn't read on the notepad.

Detective Francois's eyes narrowed to slits. "So, two days before. That was the last time you were in Ms. Sumika's house."

"Yes, that's what I said."

"And the last time you saw her was the day of the donors' open house?"

"That's right. Right before the event, Kim complained of a migraine. I had everything under control, so I told her to go home and rest."

Detective Francois cocked his head to the side and gave her a contemplative look. "That didn't seem odd to you? I mean, this donors' open house is a big deal, right?" Maggie nodded. "So suddenly Ms. Sumika is too sick to attend, and neither you nor Mr. Gustev thought that was odd?"

Maggie fought to keep her annoyance in check. Detective Francois hadn't known Kim or how devoted she was to the museum. Then again, it seemed like there was a lot she hadn't known about Kim either. She hadn't thought it was suspicious for Kim to miss the event at the time, but now… Maybe she should have paid a little more attention to Kim in the last days of her life.

"Kim suffered from migraines," she answered. "I didn't think it was suspicious that the stress of the new exhibit and the party got to her."

Detective Francois frowned. "What do you know about Ms. Sumika's finances?"

Maggie shrugged. "Nothing, really. I mean, I knew she'd inherited the house from her parents. I know how much a place like that would go for, so I assumed Kim wasn't financially strapped, even with the gambling. At least, not on paper."

The detective leaned forward. "What do you mean 'at least, not on paper'?"

Maggie found herself instinctively leaning away from the detective. She could see why he'd insisted on having this conversation in an interrogation room. It was effectively intimidating.

"I didn't mean anything. Just that houses like Kim's sell for quite a bit these days. Neither of us made a fortune working for the Larimer, but I figured Kim at least had the house as an asset."

"And your rental income."

"Yes, although she wasn't charging me anywhere near market rate."

"Right." He pulled stapled sheets of paper from between the pages of his notebook. "Have you seen this before?" He passed the pages across the table to her.

Last Will and Testament. The first paragraph looked to be standard boilerplate language with Kim's name typed onto a thick black line.

"I've never seen this before this moment, no."

Detective Francois reached for the papers and flipped the pages until he got to a section highlighted in yellow. "Please read this paragraph for me."

Maggie read, her heart picking up its pace until it was thundering as she read the last words.

Kim had left her house and all personal possessions to Maggie.

She met Detective Francois's gaze. "I didn't know."

"You had no idea you were the sole benefactor, save for a few charitable bequests, of Kim Sumika's will?"

"I had no idea, Detective. You have to believe me."

Detective Francois studied her.

She couldn't tell if he did, in fact, believe her, but she was stunned. Kim hadn't even hinted about the arrangements she'd made. Maggie knew she'd been an only child, but she recalled Kim speaking about a cousin in Indiana. Heck, she was surprised her friend even had a will. She'd only had one drawn up after Ellison had died without any instructions regarding his final wishes. Since they were divorced by then, she hadn't had any say in how his property was distributed. She'd heard his sister got everything, but it hadn't been her place to inquire.

Detective Francois took the will from her and slid it back between the pages of his notebook. "One of your other colleagues mentioned that there was a group that wasn't happy with the Larimer exhibiting the Viperé ruby. They staged a protest in front of the museum several weeks ago."

The sudden change in topic was jarring. She just looked at the detective for a moment.

"Yes," she answered finally. "Ah, the Art and Antiquities Repatriation Project people. They've staged protests at various museums in California and elsewhere against exhibits that show items that are the subject of cultural or repatriation claims."

"Are you a member of this organization or any similar organization?"

Maggie frowned. "No."

"Several of the board members I spoke with mentioned that you'd made an impassioned argument against the Larimer mounting this exhibit. Why is that?"

She didn't try to hide her irritation this time. "I wasn't arguing against the exhibit. I just thought that the board should be aware of and prepared for the fact that not everyone was going to agree with a decision to exhibit the Viperé."

"Huh." He tapped his pen against the notepad. "And did you agree with the board's decision to move forward?"

"I didn't disagree. It's a complex issue, as evidenced by the various lawsuits."

The detective leaned forward in his seat. "So you sympathize with the plaintiffs in these lawsuits and organizations like the one that was protesting your museum."

"I do," she gritted out, regretting her decision to speak with the detective without a lawyer.

It was clear that Detective Francois wasn't broadening the scope of the investigation. He was narrowing it. On her.

She reached for her purse at her feet. "Detective, I don't think I wish to answer any more questions without an attorney."

Detective Francois spread his hands out. "Ms. Scott, I'm just trying to get to the bottom of the crimes that seem to be swirling around you."

She stood, her chair scraping against the linoleum flooring. "And I hope you do get to the bottom of these crimes. For Kim's sake. But I promise you, when you do, I won't be the person you find there."

His expression clearly said he didn't believe that, but he stood and opened the door for her.

She marched down the short hallway leading away from the interrogation rooms and toward the front exit. She came to a stop just past the front reception area.

Kevin was leaning against the side wall, his arms crossed over his chest.

He straightened when he saw her.

"What are you doing here?" she asked, approaching

warily. Guilt gnawed at her. She didn't regret the choice she'd made in not telling him about her miscarriage when it happened, but it had been unkind to drop it on him like she had.

"I heard Detective Francois brought you in for questioning." He took a step closer to her.

"Do I want to know how you knew that?"

"I have my spies." He gave her a tepid smile. "Are you ready to get out of here?"

She definitely was, but they had so much they needed to talk about, and she wasn't in the right headspace to tackle it at the moment.

"It might be best if I get an Uber. I know we have things we need to talk about, and we will, but I just can't right now."

Kevin held his hands up. "I'm just offering you a ride home. We don't have to speak at all if you don't want."

She hesitated for a moment more before her shoulders relaxed and she returned his tepid smile with one of her own. "Okay then, thank you. A ride would be great."

He led her out the front doors of the police station and to the parking lot. The farther they got from the station, the more she relaxed.

"Do you mind if I ask you what Detective Francois asked you in there?"

She looked up at him, her throat constricting with fear. "He thinks I killed Kim. He pretty much said as much." She stopped walking, and Kevin paused alongside her. The man walking behind them shot them a dirty look and veered around them. "Kevin, Detective Francois had Kim's will, and she left me everything."

Kevin stroked his chin. "And I take it you had no idea she was going to do this."

"None at all." She pulled him to the side, out of the path of another pedestrian heading their way. "I mean, I knew Kim didn't have much family to speak of, but I never expected her to name me in her will."

Kevin's eyes darkened. "And because she did, it now looks like you had a motive for wanting her dead."

She nodded. "That seems to be what the detective is thinking. Kevin, I'm scared. Detective Francois isn't looking at anyone else. He thinks I did this. The theft and killing Kim."

He pulled her into his arms and dropped a kiss on the top of her head. "We're going to get to the bottom of this. I promise you."

Maggie wrapped her arms around him. Let his warmth seep through her. And tried to believe that he was right and that they'd find the real culprit.

Chapter Fifteen

Kevin led Maggie toward his Mustang. Tess had called him less than an hour earlier with the contact information for Josh Huber, head of the organization that had staged the protest against the Larimer Museum. She'd also informed him that Detective Francois had brought Maggie in for another round of questioning. He'd asked Tess to give Huber a call and set up a meeting for that afternoon and hopped in the car, headed for the police station.

Of course, the cops wouldn't let him into the interrogation room with Maggie, but he'd refused to leave. Detective Francois seemed to have homed in on Maggie as his prime suspect, and he wanted to be there if she needed support or, worse, needed someone to get her a lawyer. He'd breathed a sigh of relief when she'd walked out of the back of the police station.

But now he wasn't sure what he wanted to say to her. He was still upset with her for having kept her pregnancy from him, even if he was beginning to understand why she'd done so. More than anything, what he felt was remorse. Remorse for having not been there for her when she'd needed him. Guilt at having broken up with her at all. As much as he'd tried to convince himself that he'd had to leave everything behind and focus all his efforts and attention on football, he knew now that he'd just been scared. Scared of the intensity of his feelings for her. So he'd pushed her away. Ran away from her, actually.

But it hadn't worked. He'd never stopped thinking about her.

And now? Now that she was back in his life, he wasn't willing to let her go.

They both got in his car, but he made no move to start the engine.

"Maggie, about yesterday—"

She reached across the console for his hand. "Kevin, I'm sorry. I shouldn't have sprung the miscarriage on you like that," she interrupted.

"No, you have nothing to apologize for." He turned her hand palm up and ran his index finger along her wrist.

"I do. I was angry about losing my job and frustrated with everything that's going on right now, and I lashed out at you. I wanted to hurt you, and that was wrong."

He entwined his fingers with hers. "There are a lot of things I want to say, but I'm not sure how to say them at the moment."

"We do need to talk, but maybe right now isn't the best time. We both need time to process, and then there's this." She gestured toward the police station.

"So let's make a deal. After this—" he made the same gesture that she had toward the police station "—is all over, we'll talk. Really talk. Deal?"

She smiled at him, and his heart turned over.

"Deal," she said.

He wanted to kiss her. He always had loved kissing Maggie.

His phone beeped and he groaned inside. He pulled it from his pocket and looked at the screen. "It's a text from

Tess. She's set up a meeting for me with Josh Huber. He's the director of the Art and Antiquities Repatriation Project. The group that protested the Viperé exhibit at the Larimer. He has time to speak with me now." He looked at her with a question in his eye. "To see us now?"

"What are you waiting for?"

The Art and Antiquities Repatriation Project was housed in a rundown slip of a building that had seen better days. In fact, the entire block looked as if it had seen better days. There was a hotel on one corner, its front window so filthy the Vacancies Available sign was nearly obscured, and a corner store on the other. Several of the storefronts had signs proclaiming them For Rent, but a handful of businesses seemed to be holding on. A tarot card reader, a yoga studio and a fabric store were among them. Seeing this area, Kevin regretted bringing Maggie with him and even considered blowing the meeting off and rescheduling. But Maggie wasn't wrong about one thing: the pressure was building to give Francois anyone other than her to focus on as a suspect. And he hoped he could find that someone among the workers and volunteers at the Art and Antiquities Repatriation Project.

He parked at the curb in front of the address he had for the AARP. It took a minute for a voice to come over the intercom after he pressed the buzzer, but the door unlocked as soon as he identified himself and Maggie.

The space was uncomfortably warm bordering on sweltering, but it was clear that someone had done their best to do what they could with the AARP offices. The walls were a bright white made brighter by the recessed lighting illuminating the space. Fresh flowers sat in a vase on the desk just inside the doorway. The space was empty, save for several mismatched desks, some wood, some metal, in what was clearly a shared workspace. A number of file cabinets lined one wall, and a table in the back held a coffee maker, paper cups and other assorted items.

A man stepped out of the office at the back of the workspace. He was short, no more than five foot five or six, middle-aged and bald.

"Kevin Lombard?" The man approached them warily.

Kevin held out his hand. "Yes. And this is Maggie Scott. Thank you for meeting with us, Mr. Huber."

Josh Huber was the director of the Art and Antiquities Repatriation Project. Since he'd done his homework, Kevin knew that Huber had a degree in art history and that he'd spent more than a decade lecturing at a local college before taking on the position at the AARP. The protest at the Larimer was one of many the group had staged over the past several years. They'd seemingly had a few successes, getting a couple of museums and private collectors to donate smaller pieces to museums in the countries from which the pieces originated. But through his research into the group, he'd learned that repatriation was a tricky, costly and sometimes politically fraught endeavor.

Huber led them into his office. The space was cramped and stuffy.

"Sorry about the heat in here. Seems like no matter what I do, this office is always too hot." Huber dropped down into his office chair.

There was only one visitor's chair. He let Maggie take it and stood next to her.

"It's fine," Kevin said. "We don't want to take up too much of your time. We're hoping you can answer some questions for us."

"About our protest at the Larimer." Huber leaned back in his chair, pen in hand.

"Well, yes. I'm sure you're aware the Viperé ruby was stolen the night before last."

Huber frowned. "And you think that the Art and Antiquities Repatriation Project had something to do with that? Sorry to deprive you of an easy answer, but no way."

Maggie leaned forward in the chair. "We're not looking for an easy answer, Mr. Huber. We just want to get the ruby back."

Huber spun the pen in his hands. "I'm afraid I still can't help you. I'm not even sure I would if I could, but I can't."

"We know your organization believes that these types of items belong to the people of the countries from which they came," Kevin said.

"They do." Huber straightened. "They were stolen during periods of colonization." He pounded a fist on his desk.

Kevin caught the glance Maggie sent him. "Mr. Huber, we really aren't here to debate you on your views."

"I work at the Larimer," Maggie cut in. "I think you make some very good points, and I did articulate them to the board when they were considering whether or not to go forward with the exhibit."

Huber looked surprised. "Didn't seem to do much good though."

"From your point of view, no, I guess it didn't," Maggie conceded.

"Mr. Huber, was there anyone in your group who was particularly upset that the protest didn't have the desired effect of getting the museum to cancel the exhibit?"

Huber sighed. "Now why would I tell you that? You'll just use it to paint a target on the back of our volunteers."

"I promise you that's not what we intend to do," Maggie spoke up. "If you're aware of the ruby's theft, I'm sure you also know that one of my coworkers was found later that night having died of an overdose. I don't think it was an accident."

"You think your coworker was killed by whoever stole the ruby." Huber shook his head. "There's no way anyone associated with our group would be involved in what you're suggesting. No way."

"If that's true, then there's no harm in helping us," Kevin responded.

"Please," Maggie added when Huber continued to hesitate.

Huber sighed again. "Look, like I said, no one in this group would be involved in a theft. That would make them no better than the people who took these artifacts from their countries in the first place."

They weren't going to get names of members from this guy. Kevin wasn't surprised about that. Maybe Francois would have better luck. Still, he needed to get what he could from Huber. "What about people not associated with the Repatriation Project? There are always people who think that lawful protest simply isn't enough. Has anyone like that expressed an interest in the ruby lately?"

"You are right. There are always people who think that more…aggressive measures should be taken to address wrongs." Huber paused, thinking. "I can't think of anyone though who expressed an interest in the ruby per se."

Kevin's ears perked up at the hedge. "But you can think of someone who fits the description of the kind of person we're talking about generally."

"There was a girl, a woman, early twenties. Just out of college. Idealistic, you know the type." Huber was back spinning the pen between his fingers. "I don't know her name. She came to one of the protests we held, oh, maybe a month or two ago. Really aggressive. Said talk wasn't enough. We needed to get our hands dirty in the fight if we wanted to affect real change." Huber scoffed. "I've been doing this kind of work for more than twenty years. Maybe longer than this woman had been alive. I think my hands are plenty dirty."

"Do you know her name?" Kevin asked.

Huber shook his head. "No. She only came to the one protest. She made such a scene I had to ask her to leave. Never saw her again."

"Can you describe her?"

Huber shrugged. "Brunette, shortish hair. Not too tall."

That probably described thousands of women in the Los Angeles area, and they weren't even sure the woman was from here.

He and Maggie thanked Huber for his time and left.

"What do you think?" Maggie asked when they were back in the car.

"I think Francois will get the names of the members of the organization, but I don't think this group has the know-how to pull something like this off."

"So where does that leave us?"

Continuing to spin their wheels looking for a suspect that wasn't her. Since that was an answer he wasn't willing to give her, he started the engine and pulled away from the curb without a word.

Chapter Sixteen

Kevin glanced at the clock on his bedside table: 11:10 p.m. He sighed and climbed out of bed. Maybe some calming mint tea would help him finally get some sleep.

He couldn't stop thinking about Maggie.

He hoped she was getting more rest than he was, although he doubted it. Even though she insisted she wasn't going to be run out of her home, he'd seen the fear in her eyes. Everything inside of him wanted to make her feel safe.

He'd crossed the line from professional to personal the moment he'd kissed her on her front porch. Scratch that. He'd crossed that line the moment he'd realized she was the curator who had been attacked during the theft of the Viperé ruby. From that moment on, he'd wanted nothing more than to catch the man who'd put his hands on his Maggie and make him pay.

His Maggie.

That was how he used to think about her all the time. He wasn't sure when he started thinking about her like that again, but sometime in the last several days, he had. And he realized something else. He wanted another chance with her. Now he just had to figure out a way to convince her to give him one.

He glanced at the phone, wondering if it was too late to call. Of course it was. But he wasn't sure he could wait until the more socially acceptable time the next morning.

It wasn't just the nearly uncontrollable desire to at least hear her voice. This case, everything about it, bothered him.

The theft, Maggie being attacked and the threat against her, Kim Sumika's murder and now Carter Tutwilder's possible inquiries into buying a gem like the Viperé only weeks before it was stolen. None of it made sense. Especially not the attacks on Maggie. If the thief was the same person who'd made the threat against her, why had he hung around to do so? And if the thief and the person threatening Maggie weren't the same person? He wasn't sure what that would mean, and he didn't like not having answers. Not when it came to Maggie's safety.

There were simultaneously too many clues and not enough. Carter Tutwilder had been keeping something from them, he was sure of that, but was his secret relevant or just something the billionaire didn't want to see in the papers? Kim Sumika had a gambling problem, but so did thousands of other Los Angelenos. It might not have anything to do with the theft or her murder. And if Kim had reached out to Kovalev to be her new bookie, Kim would have brought real trouble down on her head by not paying up. But the timing was just too coincidental for him to shake off.

The tea kettle whistled. He poured the tea into a travel mug and carried it to his bedroom to change.

Midnight might be too late for a phone call, but nothing was stopping him from taking a drive by Maggie's house to make sure all was quiet there.

MOONLIGHT WAS STILL peeking around the edges of the blinds when she opened her eyes. She'd gone to bed at ten, exhausted. The dream she'd been having involved her and Kevin walking hand in hand on a beach, which had led to a romantic dinner, which had led to the two of them in bed. It had felt so real she almost expected to see Kevin lying in bed beside her, but of course he wasn't there. She touched the cold spot next to her with longing before chiding herself. She couldn't fall back into things with Kevin.

A shadow shifted outside her window. She stilled, her heart in her throat. A long minute passed and she relaxed. Just shadows.

The last several days had put her on edge, and she hated it. Hated looking over her shoulder all the time. Hated feeling unsafe in her own home. And it didn't feel like she and Kevin were getting any closer to discovering who was behind the theft of the ruby, Kim's death or the terror campaign against her.

Something caught her eye outside the window. It wasn't just a shadow. There was someone out there. A glance at the clock showed that it was 11:25 p.m. No one with good intentions would be lurking around her house at this time of the night.

She slid from her bed as quietly as she could, her heart in her throat.

Grabbing her cell phone, she moved into the living room, not turning on any lights. As long as the person outside thought she was still asleep, she had the element of surprise.

She waited impatiently, her eyes moving from the windows at the front of the house to the ones in the back, looking for any movement, as Kevin's phone rang. After what seemed like hours, he picked up.

"There's someone here," she whispered frantically as soon as the call connected.

"I'm two minutes away." She wondered how he could already be so close, but any thought of asking the question was cut off by the sound of the glass pane in her back door shattering.

She dropped the phone and lunged for the end table in the living room where she kept a Maglite flashlight.

"Maggie? Maggie, are you there? Answer me, Maggie."

She grabbed the flashlight, which was heavy enough to double as a weapon if it came to that, and clicked it on. She turned the light toward the back door just as the hand jutting into the house through the broken pane found the lock and turned it. She jerked the beam toward the intruder's face.

He wore a mask, but this one was different from the one the thief at the Larimer wore. It covered the top of the intruder's head and his neck and came up to his nose, but left his forehead and eye area uncovered. Something tugged at the back of her mind for a fleeting moment, but the intruder's startled jerk chased it away.

"The cops are on their way, and I have a gun. If you come any closer, I will shoot." She could only hope the intruder couldn't hear the lie in her voice.

Luck was on her side. A pounding sounded on the front door as the last words left her mouth.

"Maggie!" Kevin yelled.

"I'm okay," she shouted back. "He's at the back door."

The intruder's eyes went wide. He pulled his hand out of the door and lurched away.

She waited several seconds before going to the door and peering out of what was left of the window.

The intruder hoisted himself over the back fence and disappeared into the darkness of the neighbor's lawn.

Kevin rounded the side of the cottage.

She jerked the damaged door open and pointed at the house behind the cottage. "He went over the fence."

Kevin looked her up and down quickly.

"I'm fine. He didn't make it inside."

"Call 911, tell them you had an intruder and ask them to call Detective Francois," he said before taking off after the intruder.

Into the darkness.

KEVIN WAITED UNTIL he saw Maggie slip back into the house and the door close. Then he headed for the back fence, vaulting over it with one hand, his gun in the other. The neighbor's yard was shrouded in darkness. The little bit of illumination came from the bulb over the neighbor's back door and created eerie shadows and shapes. He froze, listening for the sound of an animal bigger than the usual night creatures moving about. For several long moments, all he heard were the chirps of crickets. Then, almost as if they were warning him of impending danger, the chirping to his right fell silent.

He turned in that direction and saw the shadow moving quickly along the side of the porch toward the front of the house. He started for it, but the man must have seen or heard him coming.

The intruder took off running.

Kevin gave chase.

The intruder didn't seem to be worried about being quiet or stealthy anymore. He just wanted to get away now. And he was fast. In a matter of seconds, he'd managed to put a good distance between them.

It struck him that the intruder seemed familiar with the neighborhood. Was that because he'd been staking out Maggie's home or could there be another reason? He'd be sure to ask, as soon as he had the man in custody.

He picked up his pace, trying to close the distance. Even though the sun had long since set, the night was warm, leaving him sweaty even though he'd only run two blocks. He kept in shape, running several miles every week. But his heart was pounding, and the adrenaline rushing through his body wasn't helping him pace himself. And he was worried about Maggie. What if the intruder was leading him on a wild-goose chase just to get him away from her house? He could have a partner or double back. Maggie was all alone. Where the hell was the patrol that was supposed to be keeping an eye on her house?

Coming to the corner, Kevin turned in the direction he'd seen the intruder flee. The street and sidewalk were empty.

"Damnit." The intruder couldn't have disappeared.

He hadn't heard the sound of an engine turning, so he doubted the person had escaped in a car. He scanned the street.

A thick hedge ran along the property line of a nearby house.

Kevin crossed to it; it was dark, but it only took him seconds to find the narrow path leading between two neighboring houses. The shadow at the end of the path turned in time for Kevin to catch the whites of the man's eyes before he darted away again.

Propelled by a new surge of adrenaline, he raced down the path after the man. He had to catch the intruder and put an end to him terrorizing Maggie.

He got to the end of the path and found himself surrounded by trees. The path had ended at what appeared to be the beginning of a wooded area behind the homes. Maggie's intruder could be anywhere. Hiding among the trees. It wouldn't be safe for him to plunge into the thicket.

A moment too late, he sensed someone behind him.

Before he could turn, something hit him hard over the back of his head.

He went down to his knees, dizzy, stars flashing behind his eyes. Thankfully, he didn't lose consciousness. He could hear footfalls heading back down the path. He struggled to his feet, disoriented and woozy.

The footsteps faded into silence.

Chapter Seventeen

When he arrived back at Maggie's house, she was already speaking to one of the police officers that had responded to her call while the other officer searched around the perimeter of the house. Detective Francois arrived minutes later, and Maggie described the attempted break-in, with Kevin taking over the tale once the foot chase began. Francois sent the officers out to scour the neighborhood, but Kevin wasn't surprised when they returned without having spotted the intruder.

"Do you need to get checked out at the hospital, Lombard?" Francois asked.

Kevin rubbed the back of his head where he'd been hit. There was a little bump there, but he'd had worse. "I'll be fine."

Francois gave him a look that said he disagreed with his decision, but he didn't push. "Ms. Scott, the police department is doing everything it can to get to the bottom of the current situation, but it appears we are dealing with someone who wants to hurt you and who may have already killed Kim Sumika. I'd strongly advise you to stay with a friend for a while. Just until we have a better handle on the situation."

Maggie made a face. "I could ask my friend Lisa, but

her place is an hour away and small. And she has a cat that hates me." She shook her head, seemingly rejecting the idea even as she mentioned it.

"You can stay with me." Warning bells went off in his head immediately. Having her only feet away from his bed was probably not the best idea he'd ever had. Not when he couldn't have her in his bed. But he could see she was afraid, and he could keep his libido in check if that was what it took to make her feel safe.

"I don't know," she said hesitantly.

"I do. I have a guest room. It's yours for as long as you want it."

She gave him a grateful smile. "Thank you."

He waited while Maggie packed a bag and locked up the cottage. She didn't want to be stranded without a car, so she followed him to his place in her own car. When they got there, he ran inside the apartment building to get her a visitor's parking permit, then called Tess and updated her on the night's events as Maggie pulled into one of the reserved spaces while he kept an eye out.

"None of this is making a whole lot of sense," Tess said when he'd finished his update.

"On that, we agree."

"Well, I do have some news that's good. My source was able to get a location on Ivan Kovalev. He's partying at the bar he owns, Nightingale's. My source says the way the booze and recreational drugs are flowing, Ivan is likely to be there until closing at four. The source can get you into the club, but he can't guarantee Ivan will meet with you."

"But Ivan knows I want to speak with him?"

"Oh, he knows. There isn't much Ivan doesn't know. Once you're in the club, if Ivan is open to talking to you, he'll find you."

Kevin watched as Maggie got out of her car and went to the trunk for her overnight bag. "The timing sucks. Maggie is going to stay with me for a while. I want to get her settled, and I'm not sure about leaving her alone."

"We know where Ivan is going to be tonight. I can send someone else if you really can't make it, but you know the details of this case back and forth."

And he didn't want to leave Ivan's questioning to anyone else. Finding out what he knew might be the key to figuring out what was going on and stopping it. Maggie was heading for him now. He glanced at his watch: 12:18 a.m. That gave him time to get Maggie settled, wait till she fell asleep and head to the club.

"And you're sure he's going to be at Nightingale's?" Kevin asked.

Maggie stopped in front of him and waited.

"That's what the source said."

"Okay, got it. Maggie is here. I've got to go." He ended the call.

"Who was that?" Maggie asked.

"Tess." He slid her bag from her shoulder and tossed it over his own. "I was filling her in on the attempted break-in at your house and you staying with me for a while."

"I don't know if it will be awhile. Let's just take it one day at a time."

"Whatever you want. You ready to go up?" He led her to the elevators into the building.

"I heard you and Tess talking about Nightingale's. That's that trendy club in Hollywood where all the celebrities hang out right? Who is going to be there tonight? Clooney? Pitt? One of the many, many Chrises?" Maggie asked jokingly after the elevator doors closed and they'd started their ascent.

"Tess's informant got a location on Ivan Kovalev. He owns Nightingale's, a club in Hollywood."

"Are we going to talk to him?"

Kevin raised his hands. "Ivan Kovalev is a dangerous man. I don't want you anywhere near him."

Maggie frowned. "He may have answers to who killed Kim and is trying to destroy my life."

"I get it, but we have to be careful. Your safety is my number one priority."

"Kevin—"

The elevator stopped on the twelfth floor, and the doors slid open.

"We don't have to speak to Ivan tonight. Tess said he's at the club nearly every night." He felt a moment of guilt about the white lie then shook it off, remembering that, while she may not have lied to him, she'd kept a pretty major piece of information from him. At least he was doing it to protect her.

He could tell from her deepening frown that she didn't like that answer, but she nodded.

They got off the elevator, and he led her to a door at the end of the hallway.

He opened the door, flicked on the light and led her into the space.

"You have a nice place," Maggie said, her eyes roaming over the space.

"Tanya found it for me. It's five minutes from the hospital, which is its best feature. At least, in her opinion."

Maggie shot him a wan smile.

"You have to be exhausted. The guest room is just down this way." He led her down the short hallway to the left of the front door.

His guest bedroom wasn't much, just a bed, dresser

and nightstand, but it was warm and comfortable, and she'd be safe in his place.

He set her bag down at the foot of the bed and stepped back into the hall.

Maggie touched his arm as he passed by her, sending sparks of electric desire through him.

"Thank you," she said softly.

He pressed a kiss to her forehead then stepped back. He'd wanted to do much more, but she needed to rest. "You don't ever have to thank me. I'll always be there when you need me."

He retreated to his own room but didn't change into pajamas. He knew she'd be angry with him, but there was no way he was going to take her to Ivan's club. Especially when he wasn't sure Ivan wasn't behind everything that had been happening. He just had to wait for her to go to sleep, and then he could slip out of the apartment.

He heard Maggie's bedroom door open and her footsteps as she headed for the single bathroom in the apartment. She took a long shower then he heard the bathroom door open and the floor creak as she headed back to her room.

The bedroom door snapped shut, and the apartment fell quiet.

He lay back on his bed, planning to wait a few minutes for her to fall asleep before he left. While he waited, he ran through the events of the night in his head. The attempt to break into Maggie's home was bold, and it had terrified him. Whoever was behind everything that was happening seemed to be obsessed with Maggie. And obsessions only ended one of two ways. The person was caught or the object of the obsession was eliminated.

Fear and fury burned in his chest.

He would not let anything happen to Maggie.

The sound of the guest room door creaking open sent him on instant alert. Light spilled out of the guest bedroom. He sat up in bed, watching as Maggie's shadow moved closer and closer to his room.

She crept forward, headed for the bathroom, he guessed.

Maggie continued to creep forward, but not to the bathroom. She stopped at his bedroom door. "Kevin?"

"You okay?"

"I can't sleep."

He swung his bare feet to the floor. "I can make you some tea. Something soothing that might help you fall asleep."

She came into the room, and he got a good look at her. She was wearing a satin nightie that hugged her plump breasts and showed miles of long silky leg.

His lower body sprung to attention.

She stepped up to the side of the bed, her thigh brushing against him. "I was thinking about something else that might help me sleep."

"Maggie." His voice came out low and rough. He was surprised he was able to form words with her standing so close. So nearly naked. "This might not be a good idea."

But even as he spoke, he couldn't help reaching out and drawing his hand lightly over Maggie's hip.

"I don't want to think about rubies or death or tomorrow. I just want right now. With you."

She lowered her mouth to his, and his control snapped.

The years, the fears, the secrets, they all melted away with that kiss. All that was left was desire.

With those words, he closed the remaining distance between them, capturing her lips in a fervent kiss.

It was as if time hadn't passed at all. Her mouth claimed

his, her tongue exploring with hunger. She kissed him like a woman desperate.

He knew the feeling because he felt it too.

Her hands rose and pressed against his chest, coaxing him back on the bed. He let her take the lead. She straddled him, and it was a fight not to lose control.

How many nights had he dreamed of this? Too many to count.

He wrapped his hands around her hips, pulling her against the hardness and heat between his thighs. He wanted her to feel how much he wanted her. To feel the weight of his arousal.

Her mouth left his, but her hold on him remained firm. She began a sensual exploration down his neck, her tongue caressing and igniting a thunderous beat in his chest and ears.

There were countless reasons why he should pull away. But he curled around her hips, fitting her tightly against him.

As if she sensed his hesitation, she whispered in his ear, "I want this. I need you."

What little control he had left shattered. Kevin flipped them so she was under him. He kissed her with raw desire, unchecked by any more reservations.

Already shirtless, he removed his pants, letting them fall to the floor.

A soft gasp escaped her lips.

He tugged on the hem of her nightie, pulling it over her head.

It joined his pants on the floor.

He took her breast into his mouth, tasting her. As his tongue caressed her, she arched toward him, eager.

The events of the past and the last several days vanished, leaving only desire.

He kissed a scorching trail down her stomach, causing her breath to catch.

He reached for the nightstand next to his bed, where he kept protection. The next time, and there would be a next time, they'd go slow, but right now...right now he had to sink into her or he felt like he might explode from pent-up need.

After sheathing himself, he settled between her thighs, entering her slowly so she had time to adjust to every inch of him.

Seated fully, he gazed down at the woman beneath him.

Her eyes burned with passion.

"You are so beautiful," he said huskily.

"Kevin," she moaned.

Their eyes locked.

He withdrew and thrust into her, hard and fast. He withdrew again and plunged again, the rhythm desperate, greedy. The need had swelled too rapidly for him to hold back.

Her legs wrapped around him, her nails digging into his shoulders as their pleasure surged and intensified.

Their bodies met again and again.

He kissed her, caressed her, driving her to the precipice of desire—

And then her release crashed over her, and she gasped his name, her release unleashing his own.

He had expected pleasure. But this...this was something beyond his wildest imagination.

The world spun away as her body quivered under him, waves of ecstasy rippling through her. He was there with her, growling out her name, holding her just as tightly as she held him as pleasure consumed him.

He lifted his body, supporting his weight, and gazed down at her. "Are you okay?"

She leaned up, and he was amazed that his arousal surged again. She swept her lips over his and said, "No thinking. Tonight, there is only this."

Chapter Eighteen

Maggie woke up alone in Kevin's bed.

"Kevin?"

Only silence answered her.

She rose and padded from the bedroom. The kitchen and living room were empty. She glanced out of the front window of the house, her suspicions rising. Kevin's car wasn't in the driveway where he'd parked it.

Then she remembered the earlier call from Tess. Her ire peaked. She had a pretty good idea where Kevin had gone. She was happy she'd followed him to his place in her own car.

She pulled up the address for Nightingale's on her phone and got dressed. The club looked nice, upscale, not the kind of place where she could wear the jeans and sweater she'd arrived at Kevin's house in. Luckily, she'd had the foresight to pack a dress that was nice enough for a night out.

Foresight or wishful thinking? She'd seen the dress, one of her favorites because it hugged and gave in all the right places, while packing, and a thought had flashed through her mind. Her in the dress sitting across from Kevin at a candlelit table. Ridiculous under the circumstances, but she'd thrown the dress in her bag just in case.

She put it on then hopped into her car. She didn't know exactly how much of a head start Kevin had on her, but the restaurant wasn't far from his house.

She made a right turn and noticed that the dark SUV behind her did the same.

She told herself to relax, that it didn't mean anything. The driver could be going in the same direction.

She made a left at the light, and the SUV did the same. She made another left and the next immediate left. The SUV followed.

Okay, that wasn't a coincidence. There was no reason for the SUV to circle the block unless it was following her.

Her phone rang and she started, tapping the break. The SUV fell back but continued to follow her as she drove. She reached for the phone with one hand, the other still on the wheel.

"What do you think you're doing?" Kevin's voice boomed from the phone.

"What are you—"

"You didn't think I'd leave you without protection, did you? One of the other operatives from West Investigations was watching the house. He said you took off in your car before he could stop you."

She glanced at the rearview mirror. "Is that who's following me?"

"Yes. Pull over," he demanded. "I'm a block away."

She pulled to a stop at the curb, as did the SUV. It was less than a minute before Kevin's black Mustang rolled to a stop behind the SUV.

He stopped at the driver's side of the SUV and said a few words to the driver before heading for her car.

Maggie stepped out, slamming the door behind her. "Who do you think you are? Sending me off to bed like a child and then sneaking out of the house like some sneaky sneak."

Okay, so it wasn't the strongest admonition, but she was a novice at telling someone off.

Kevin looked angry, but she thought she saw the ends of his mouth tip up slightly, which only stoked her ire.

She poked him in the chest. "I am not a child. Kim was my friend, and the Viperé ruby was my responsibility. I am a part of this whether you want me to be or not. I'm not going to hide from this maniac, no matter how much—"

The rest of her rant was cut off by Kevin's lips crushing against her mouth.

For several long moments, she was lost in his kiss. Finally, Kevin stepped back.

She shook the fog of his kiss from her head. "If you think that's going to stop me from going—"

Kevin held up his hand. "I know nothing is going to stop you." He caressed her cheek with the pad of his thumb. "Nothing ever stops you from doing what you think is right. It's one of the things I lo—"

This time it was she who pressed her mouth to his. She wasn't ready to hear what he was about to say.

She pulled back after a moment. "So, Nightingale's."

He took her hand. "I'll drive. I've already got someone coming to take your car back to my house. Miller will stay with your car until he gets here."

Heat crept up her neck at the realization that Miller had seen them kissing. She left the keys to her car with Miller and got into the Mustang beside Kevin.

Nightingale's looked like a typical bar. A long bar ran along one side of the space and white tableclothed tables filled in the rest in a seemingly random pattern.

Kevin led her toward the bar. They slid onto stools and ordered drinks, tonic water for him and white wine for her.

"Shouldn't we tell someone that we're here?"

"Ivan Kovalev knows when each and every person walks through his doors. Trust me, he knows we are here, and if he doesn't know already, if we give him a few minutes, he'll know who we are."

They continued to sip their drinks at the bar, exchanging a few words but mostly waiting. It seemed like forever, but it had probably only been ten or fifteen minutes when a large man with biceps the size of tree stumps and a raised scar running along the right side of his jaw appeared beside Kevin.

"Sir. Mr. Kovalev is ready to see you now."

The man turned and started away, clearly intending for Maggie and Kevin to follow him.

She slid from the barstool. Kevin palmed her elbow, angling his body between her and the man they followed.

The man led them through the bar's main area and down a narrow hallway toward the back of the building. They passed the kitchen and heard the clank of dishes and the sound of raised voices on the other side of the swinging door. Finally, the man stopped in front of a door. A private dining room.

There were no windows and the walls were dark wood paneling. With the dim lighting, the overall feel was menacing, which Maggie was sure was the point.

A circular table dominated the space, and in the seat facing the door sat a man who Maggie had no doubt was Ivan Kovalev.

He waved them into the room and toward the table without rising. "Mr. Lombard. Ms. Scott. So good of you to join me," Kovalev said as if he'd invited them to dine with him.

Kevin squeezed her elbow, in caution or as a soothing gesture, she wasn't sure.

He pulled out a chair on the opposite side of the table for her and waited until she was seated before taking the seat next to her.

Ivan Kovalev looked to be in his early sixties, maybe a little older, lean with hair that had gone more white than gray and eyes that were shrewd. If she'd passed him on the street, not knowing that he was part of the Russian mob, she would have still given him a wide berth. Everything about the man screamed he was dangerous.

A waiter hurried in with glasses of wine and a bread-basket. He set the glasses of wine in front of Maggie and Kevin—Kovalev already had a full glass—and left the breadbasket in the middle of the table before slipping back out of the room.

"Thank you for seeing us," Kevin said.

Kovalev waved a hand in dismissal. "It is nothing. I'm sure we were destined to meet at some point with you being the new head of West Security and Investigations' corporate accounts."

It was a show of power. Kovalev knew exactly who they were.

"I've been thinking about upgrading the security at my various buildings. Maybe I should give you a call."

"West would be glad to help," Kevin responded.

Kovalev smiled. "I'm sure you would. But am I incorrect in thinking you are not here to solicit my business?"

Kovalev's gaze swung to Maggie. She was used to men assessing her, but the look Kovalev swept over her was more than just a man appreciating a woman; it was predatory, and it left her feeling as if she needed a shower. Immediately. She shook off the feeling.

Out of the side of her eye, she saw Kevin's jaw tighten. He hadn't missed the way Kovalev had looked at her.

"We're here to ask about Kim Sumika," Kevin gritted out.

Kovalev shot Kevin a smile, taking pleasure over having gotten under his skin, no doubt. "Such a shame. I'm sorry for your loss." Kovalev tipped his head at Maggie.

"Thank you," she said. "It's come to our attention that Kim may have borrowed a sum of money from you. I'm hoping you can tell us more about that."

Kovalev frowned. "I'm not sure that's any of your business."

"We've made it our business," Kevin shot back.

Kovalev's frown turned into a hard scowl.

"Mr. Kovalev, please," Maggie jumped in, hoping to dispel some of the tension. "Kim was my friend. She wasn't close to the little family she had left. I'm all she had, and I feel an obligation to find out what happened to her."

Kovalev's gaze lingered on Kevin for several seconds longer then shifted to her. His face softened, but only a fraction. "Your loyalty is admirable, but maybe misguided. You should allow the police to look into these sorts of things."

Maggie shifted her gaze to the table and said softly, "Would you? If you were in my situation?"

Her words hung there for a moment, silently. She looked at Kovalev through her lashes and waited.

Finally, he spoke. "Point well taken, my dear. What would you like to know?"

Since Kovalev seemed more willing to share with her

than with Kevin, she took over the questioning. "We know Kim had a gambling problem. She'd maxed out her credit cards and a home equity line of credit, and we were told she might have borrowed money from you."

"It appears that Anthony Cauley knows more than just wine and cupcakes. Seems to know more than I've given him credit for."

Maggie sucked in a breath. The last thing she wanted to do was to get Anthony in trouble with Ivan Kovalev. She started to speak.

Kovalev waved her off. "It's nothing. People talk. Mr. Cauley is of no concern to me." He took a sip of wine before he spoke again. "Yes, Ms. Sumika owed me money. Or she did. She paid off her debt, in full, with interest, about a week before her untimely death."

Maggie shot a surprised look at Kevin. For his part, his expression remained unchanged.

"Would you mind telling us how much that was?"

Kovalev's frown returned. He was silent for a beat. "Fifty thousand dollars, give or take."

Maggie swallowed hard. That was, she knew, nearly Kim's entire salary for a year. Where did she get that kind of money?

The Viperé ruby. If she was involved, maybe the fifty thousand was her cut. Or part of it. The ruby was worth multiples of fifty thousand dollars.

"Is there anything else you'd like to know? I'm sorry but I have a busy evening ahead of me." Kovalev downed the remainder of his wine. He'd clearly lost interest in them. It was time to go.

But there was one question she wanted to ask. Something she needed to know.

She started to speak, but Kevin reached for her hand. This time, it was clear what he intended to convey.

He stood, pulling her with him. "Mr. Kovalev, thank you for your time."

Kovalev waved at them again, a clear dismissal.

Big biceps waited for them outside of the room. He led them in a reverse trek down the hall and through the bar's dining area to the door.

She guessed Kovalev didn't want them to stay for a nightcap.

The door to the bar banged closed after them.

"Why didn't you let me ask him if he'd killed Kim?"

"Because he wouldn't have told you the truth," Kevin said, his arm around her, leading her to the car. "And I already know he didn't kill Kim."

She stopped walking. "You do? How?"

"Kovalev knew who we were before we stepped foot in the bar. He knew who you were. That tells me he's done his homework, and I have no doubt that he knows you inherit Kim's estate."

She wasn't following. "So?"

"So, if Kim hadn't paid him the money she owed him, he'd have made it clear that he expected you to pay out of the money she left you. Men like Kovalev don't just let a debt die when the person who owes the debt dies, not if they can help it."

"So you think he was telling us the truth about Kim paying off her debt." Maggie let out a breath of frustration. Her prior thought about where Kim had gotten the money to pay off that debt came swimming back to her. "Which means he didn't have a motive to kill Kim or steal the ruby."

"Exactly," Kevin said, walking them to the car.

"So what now?"

Kevin pulled open the passenger-side door for her, but she made no move to get into the car.

He looked her in the eye. "Now we keep pulling threads until we find the one that unravels this whole mess."

Chapter Nineteen

Two hours after leaving Ivan Kovalev, Maggie lay in Kevin's bed, one leg slung over his, her head resting on his chest. He snored lightly, but she hadn't been able to fall asleep after they'd made love. She knew that the more time she spent in his arms, in his bed, the harder it would be to walk away from him when the time came. And it would come. No matter how electric their lovemaking or how safe she felt with him, she wasn't willing to risk her heart again. She'd tried love twice and failed both times. That was enough for her.

Repressing a sigh, she eased herself out of Kevin's arms, slipping from the bed. She wrapped herself in the quilt from the bottom of the bed and padded from the room, closing the door behind her. After a quick stop in the guest bedroom where she was supposed to be sleeping to grab her laptop, she settled onto the living room sofa.

She opened the laptop and logged on to Facebook. She'd tried to avoid the news about the Larimer, but curiosity was finally getting to her. She went to the museum's Facebook page and scanned the comments. Most of them were sympathetic, dismay and disgust about the theft the chief responses. But a few almost seemed to celebrate the ruby going missing. She scanned the thumbnail photos of the commenters, wondering if one of the posters was the aggressive brunette that Josh Huber had told them about. None of the photos jumped out at her.

She navigated to the AARP page. There were several posts about exhibits that the group was against and pictures from the many protests that they'd held. She scrolled through the posts, not sure what she was looking for. Probably nothing, but maybe mindlessly scrolling would slow her racing thoughts enough that she'd be able to go to sleep.

The last several days of her life had been nothing but chaos. One of her coworkers and closest friends was dead, quite possibly because she'd been involved in stealing the Viperé. Why hadn't Kim come to her if she was in trouble? After everything Kim had done for her since the scandal in New York, Maggie would have lent her money to get out of debt if she'd needed it. It might not have been enough, but it had to be better than borrowing from a mobster or, worse, getting involved in a major jewel theft.

If that was what Kim had done. Maggie still didn't want to believe it. She wasn't sure she would believe it until there was incontrovertible proof.

She scrolled past a photo of a protest then paused, swiping down so the photo came back onto the screen. The picture was of two young women and a young male holding protest signs. The man and one of the women were blond, but the brunette with them, she looked familiar.

Maggie clicked on the photo, and it popped up in its own browser window, filling her computer screen. The bigger picture was sharper, the faces in it clearer.

Clear enough that there was no doubt.

The brunette woman in the photo was Diyana Shelton.

MAGGIE HAD AWAKENED him at four in the morning with the photo of Diyana Shelton, the intern at the Larimer, at an AARP protest. He had to admit that she did fit the description of the young brunette that Josh Huber had given them, but he'd cautioned Maggie against jumping to any conclusions. Maggie had been ready to drive to Diyana's apartment and confront the woman before dawn. He'd convinced her to wait until a more reasonable time that morning, but just barely. At seven thirty, they headed to Diyana's apartment, hoping to catch her before she left for the day.

Maggie had given the intern a ride home several times when they'd both had to stay late working on the exhibit, so he hadn't had to tap into West Investigations' vast resources to find an address for the young woman. Diyana lived in a nondescript garden-style apartment. Each of the apartments had a balcony, and the grounds seemed to be fairly well kept. He wasn't sure how much interns made, but it must be a decent amount if Diyana was able to foot the rent here. Residents had to buzz the front door open for their guests, so their appearance at her apartment couldn't come as a complete surprise to Diyana.

Kevin pressed the button for apartment 303, the top floor of the three-floor building, and they waited. It was just after eight, and Maggie had been pretty sure that Diyana would still be at home since the intern didn't usually arrive at the museum until nine thirty.

He was about to press the buzzer again when a voice came over the intercom mounted on the outside wall.

"Yes?"

"Diyana, it's Maggie Scott and Kevin Lombard. I'm sorry to drop in on you so early in the morning, but there's something important we need to discuss with you. Can we come up?"

Diyana didn't respond, but static crackled on her end, so he knew the line was still open.

Maggie shot him a look then said, "Diyana, please."

"Okay."

The line went dead, and a moment later there was a buzz then the door unlocked.

He and Maggie took the stairs to the third floor.

Diyana waited for them outside of apartment 303, barelegged in fuzzy pink slippers, an oversized sweater wrapped around her. "What is it?"

He couldn't blame her for the irritation he heard in her voice. He wouldn't have been happy at having people drop in on him at eight in the morning on a workday. And, if Diyana had a hand in the theft of the Viperé ruby, it was likely him and Maggie showing up at her apartment at this time of the morning had spiked a bit of fear in her.

Good.

He didn't take Diyana for a criminal mastermind, which meant that fear was likely to drive her to make mistakes. And mistakes were good for him and Maggie.

"Again, I'm sorry for dropping in on you, but you know I'm not allowed at the museum, and we really do need to speak with you," Maggie said again without smiling.

Diyana shrugged, but the movement made her appear scared more than nonchalant. "Okay, so what is so urgent?"

"We might want to have this conversation inside," Kevin said.

Diyana hesitated for a moment then stepped back and let them pass into the apartment.

Maggie had printed out a copy of the photo she'd found

on Facebook. She pulled it from her purse now. "This." She handed the piece of paper over to Diyana. "That's you at a protest organized by the Arts and Antiquities Repatriation Project."

Diyana's eyes widened. She licked her lips, panic in her eyes. "So?"

"So what were you doing there?" he snapped.

She shifted her weight from one leg to the other, chewing her bottom lip. "It was a protest. Like some museum was profiting off of the stolen artifacts from Mexico."

"AARP is the group that staged the protest against us a few weeks ago."

"So?" Diyana repeated, her gaze skittering away from Maggie's.

The girl was a terrible liar.

"Look, you can tell us what you know, or I can call Detective Larimer and tell him what we know about you. I'm sure he will have no problem hauling you down to the police station."

"But I didn't do anything!"

"Then you have nothing to worry about," Maggie said.

Diyana pressed her lips together.

"Fine." The intern was working his patience. He pulled his phone from his pocket. "I'm calling Detective Francois."

"No. Don't do that." Diyana reached for his hand, stopping him from bringing the phone to his ear. "My parents will kill me if I get arrested."

"Well, you should start talking then," Kevin shot back.

Unless she'd been involved in the theft, she wasn't going to be arrested, but Detective Francois would want to talk to her anyway once Kevin told him about their visit with the intern. He didn't share that piece of information with her.

"Fine," she huffed as if she were a five-year-old. "Look, all I was going to do was add a couple of names to the guest list for the donors' open house."

Maggie's forehead furrowed. "What names?"

Diyana rolled her eyes. "I didn't do it, okay? Like, you guarded that list like it was gold or something. I knew I wouldn't be able to sneak the names onto it without you noticing, so no harm, no foul, right?" She crossed her arms over her chest defensively.

"I don't understand," Maggie said. "Whose names were you going to add to the list and why?"

"Just a couple friends of mine. They wanted to get inside the party, and when the board members and whatnot started up with the speeches about how great it was to have the Viperé ruby at the Larimer, they were going to chant and stuff. Like just civil disobedience."

"What are these friends' names?" Kevin asked.

Diyana pressed her lips together again.

He waved his phone at her. "Detective Francois is not going to ask as nicely."

"Fine." She gave him two names. "You're making a big deal out of nothing. I couldn't get their names on the list, so the protest didn't happen."

"But the theft of the Viperé did," Maggie pointed out.

Diyana held her hands out in a surrender pose. "Hey, my friends had nothing to do with that. All they were going to do was, like, yell a little until security dragged them out. That's it."

If her friends were anything like Diyana, Kevin doubted very much they'd know the first thing about stealing a precious jewel. "Were you and your friends members of the AARP?"

Diyana shrugged. "We were but they do their own thing mostly now."

"Why did they leave the group?" Maggie followed up.

Diyana snorted. "I mean, Josh has been doing this work for, like, twenty years, and he isn't exactly getting it done. They felt like they could do better on their own."

"And you?" Maggie said. "Why did you leave the group? Or did you?"

Diyana shrugged again. "I don't know. I mean, I think that these artifacts should go back where they belong, but I also want to be a curator someday."

Welcome to adulthood, he wanted to say. One hard choice after another.

"Are you going to tell Robert what I almost did?" Diyana looked at Maggie with a plea in her eyes.

"I'm on leave from the museum right now, but I really think you should tell Robert. I can't promise you that things will work out for you the way you want them to, but I know that it would show a lot of maturity and integrity if you did. I think Robert would appreciate that."

Diyana chewed her bottom lip. "Maybe."

They left the young woman contemplating her next move.

"Are you going to tell your boss about Diyana's actions?" Kevin asked Maggie once they'd stepped back outside.

"Well, since I'm on administrative leave, I don't think there is any conflict in giving her a little time to work up the courage to do it herself. But if she doesn't—" Maggie nodded "—yeah, I'll have to."

"I think she was telling us the truth," he said, holding the passenger-side door open for Maggie.

She let out a deep, frustrated breath. "Yeah, unfortunately for me, I do too."

Chapter Twenty

Maggie followed Kevin into his house. She could feel a panic attack coming on. Her throat constricted, her lungs burning from a lack of oxygen. Kevin wanted to speak with the people Diyana had planned to get into the donors' open and confirm their alibis, but Maggie's gut told her that no graduate students were behind the Viperé's theft and Kim's death. And the two were connected. She was absolutely sure of that.

No. The things that were happening now had been orchestrated by someone who'd meticulously planned it out. Planned it to seem as if she'd played a part in the theft and in killing her friend.

She tossed her purse on Kevin's kitchen table and collapsed into a chair.

Breathe. Breathe. She gulped in air.

Kevin slid into the chair next to her. "Maggie, I know this is tough for you, but don't give up hope."

She stared into Kevin's eyes. "I don't know how much more of this I can take."

"Hey." He reached across the table for her hand. "You are one of the toughest people I know. You can do this. We are going to prove your innocence."

"How? Every lead turns into a dead end. Nothing

makes any sense. If the person who stole the Viperé ruby is behind this, why kill Kim? Why stick around and leave that note for me at the office?"

"I don't know, but we will figure it out." He squeezed her hand. "You're going to make yourself sick if you don't de-stress some. Why don't you take a swim?" He slanted his head toward the sliding glass doors and the pool in the backyard beyond.

Maggie shook her head. "I don't have a swimsuit."

"There should be a couple swimsuits in the dresser in the guest room. Tanya bought a few suits to keep here, and she's never used any of them. You two are about the same size."

She looked longingly at the crystal blue water in the pool. She loved swimming, although she rarely found the time to make it to the pool at her gym. Actually, she couldn't remember the last time she made it to the gym at all.

"Are you sure Tanya wouldn't mind me stealing one of her swimsuits?"

Kevin smiled and her heart did a flip-flop. "I'm sure Tanya won't even notice. And while you swim, I'll whip us up a late breakfast. I have to go into the office at some point this morning, but you're welcome to stay here as long as you want."

"Thanks. I'm not sure what I'll do with my time now that I don't have a job to go to. I guess I need to go to my place and check on the cottage."

"If what Francois said about Kim's will is true, the cottage and Kim's house are yours now. You'll have some decisions to make whether or not you go back to the Larimer."

A knot formed in her throat. No matter what happened,

her life was never going to be the same again. She found Kevin's gaze and held it. No, too much had changed and too many feelings she'd thought were dead had been resurrected. Kevin was back in her life, and as much as she wanted to protect herself from the kind of hurt she'd felt when he'd walked away years ago, she could feel herself falling for him again. Falling just as hard as she'd fallen as a twenty-year-old coed, and she wasn't sure she had the strength to stop falling in love with him again.

She wasn't sure she wanted to stop falling in love with him again.

Maggie rose and went to the guest room, where her suitcase lay open on the bed just as she'd left it. A reminder that she hadn't slept in the guest bed at all the night before.

Memories of the prior night in Kevin's arms floated back at her as she changed into a swimsuit and headed out to the pool. The six-foot privacy fence on Kevin's side of the property line was buffeted by evergreen trees that towered at least three feet higher, giving the backyard the feel of a remote oasis.

She'd found a swim cap and goggles in the drawer, along with several swimsuits with tags still attached. She adjusted the swim cap and pulled the goggles down over her eyes before pushing off the side and gliding into the water. The water was surprisingly warm, and by the third lap, she could feel some of the stress she'd been carrying in her body easing. By the tenth lap, she was in a zone where there was nothing but the sound of the water and her breathing.

She knew the moment Kevin stepped out onto the patio. She finished her current lap then waded to the side of the pool. She pulled herself up and out. An innocuous move, but she watched desire flare in Kevin's eyes. He stood next to the chaise longue, backlit by the light coming from inside the house. His chest and feet were bare, a pair of nylon shorts hung low on his hips.

He grabbed the towel she'd left on the lounger and padded barefoot toward her. He dropped the towel over her shoulder then lowered his head and captured her mouth in a smoldering kiss that heated every inch of her skin.

His hands wandered to her hips, pulling her against him so she could feel how much he wanted her. She wanted him too. Even if she knew she shouldn't. Even if she knew it wouldn't last. She wanted him, and that was all that mattered at that moment.

He walked them toward the chaise and sat, pulling her onto his lap. The intensity of his kiss stole her breath. She thought she might like to kiss him forever. But then he pressed his hips to her, grinding against her core, and she wanted to do much more than kiss.

He shifted and flipped her so she lay on her back underneath him on the lounger.

She spread her legs wider, giving him space to seat himself comfortably against her.

She rubbed against him, rotating her hips, creating a delicious friction between their bodies. She rubbed her hands along his spine and broad shoulders, then down lower over the curve of his back to his firm behind.

His hands slipped under her bikini top. He kneaded her breast and pinched her nipple hard, sparking a pain that only heightened her pleasure. He moved on to her other breast, replaying the same movements.

It felt so good to have his weight on her body. His hands on her body. His mouth on her body.

They'd never had any problems in the bedroom. Their

physical attraction had always been explosive. This was the part they always got right, she reminded herself. It was all the other stuff that they'd struggled with.

Kevin slid his hand under the fabric of her bikini bottom, stroking her core, and she stopped thinking at all and just felt. And it felt good.

She let out a little mewling sound, and Kevin smiled sexily in return.

His gaze slid down her body. He untied her bikini top and lavished each of her breasts with kisses now that they were free. His mouth on her sent sparks shooting through her.

He slid down her body, pulling the strings that held her bottoms together. Lifting her slightly, he pulled the bottom of her bathing suit free and tossed it on top of her bikini top. She flexed her hips, enjoying the sensation of the bulging erection under his shorts.

He groaned, his jaw tightening. "Maggie, you feel so good."

"I'd feel a lot better if you weren't wearing so many clothes."

He reared up, pulling protection from his pocket before shedding his shorts.

She marveled for a moment at his hardened body and his thick erection before reaching out to pull him back down to her.

Kevin fit his hips between her legs, his length against her thigh. He held her gaze as he inched inside of her, setting a slow rhythm that sent her heart racing. His tongue darted in and out of her mouth, mimicking the pace set by the thrusting of their hips in time with each other.

He increased his rhythm, surging in and out of her until her orgasm hit with a force she'd never experienced before. She panted, clinging to him as pleasure sparked through every inch of her body. She clung to him, her legs wrapped tightly around his waist.

Kevin didn't stop making love to her. He increased his pace, pushing her toward a second orgasm that threatened to be even more powerful than the first.

His body tensed in time with hers. They quivered in each other's arms, tipping over the precipice of ecstasy together.

KEVIN STRODE THROUGH the doors of West Security and Investigations' West Coast offices the next morning, shooting a smile at the receptionist and heading for his office. He'd been reluctant to leave Maggie alone, but he needed to give Tess an update on the Larimer case and to check on several other cases that he'd been neglecting while he'd been focused on Maggie. Making love had been a much needed stress release for both of them, but he knew that neither of them would be able to completely relax until they'd cleared her name. And Maggie was right about one thing: they were really no closer to doing that than they'd been when he'd started the investigation.

He wasn't surprised to see Tess's head pop around his doorframe before he'd even booted up his computer.

She gave a perfunctory knock on the frame, the keys in her hand jingling, before speaking. "Morning, Kevin. Do you have a moment to give me an update on Maggie's case?"

He waved his boss into the office. "Of course. I was planning on stopping by your office in a minute or two anyway."

He'd been keeping Tess updated via quick calls and text messages throughout the investigation, but now he filled in all the details he'd skirted over in those prior communications. He also told his boss about Maggie having found a photograph of Diyana at one of the Art and Antiquities Repatriation Project's protests and the graduate students' thwarted plans to protest at the donors' open.

Tess massaged her temples. "This is a real mess."

"There's a logic to it," Kevin said, feeling his own frustration bubbling in his chest. "At least to our thief and killer. We just have to figure out what it is."

"I think it's safe to say that the theft of the Viperé ruby is certainly connected to Kim Sumika's death. Given the woman's gambling debt, it must have crossed your mind that she could have had a hand in the theft."

Kevin sighed. "It has, although I've been reluctant to share those thoughts with Maggie. But Kim had the same access to the ruby as Maggie did, and I do find it strange that Kim would miss the donors' open house."

"Migraines can be debilitating," Tess said, playing devil's advocate.

"Yeah," Kevin responded, his tone indicating that he still didn't buy it.

"Maggie seems to believe her friend and fellow curator was telling the truth about the migraine, and we don't have any direct evidence to the contrary. Although…" Tess shot him a pointed look. "Maggie is definitely too close to this case. I've given you wide latitude here, but do you think we should be letting her have a role in this investigation?"

"I don't think we have much of a choice. She's not going to sit back and stay out of it, and I don't think it's in her or our interest to have her out there trying to conduct her own investigation."

"Definitely not."

"She's been a help. Her dealer contact led us to Carter Tutwilder."

Tess twirled the keys. "Yeah, but so far I haven't been able to dig up anything on him that would suggest he had anything to do with the theft or Kim Sumika's death."

"He has the money to hire someone to pull this kind of thing off."

"Yeah, and if he hired someone, you can bet the money trail is buried under dozens of layers. We'll never find it."

Kevin let out a frustrated sigh. "The same could be said about Ivan Kovalev, although shockingly I believed Ivan when he said that Kim paid off her debt."

"He doesn't have a reason to lie." Tess's keys jingled, twirled and jingled again.

"No, he doesn't. But that raises another question. Where did Kim get the money to pay off the loan from Ivan?"

"And we're back to the ruby's theft," Tess said, catching the keys in the air and leaning forward in the chair. "If Kim had a hand in stealing the ruby, maybe she used her cut of the money to pay off her debt."

"And then what? Whoever she was working with killed her?"

Tess shrugged. "It wouldn't be the first time. No honor among thieves and all that."

He couldn't deny he had thought about this scenario. Heck, it was the one that made the most sense so far. Maggie was going to hate it, but it seemed clear that Kim Sumika had some role in stealing the Viperé ruby. How exactly that had led to her death was still an open question.

Tess leaned back in her chair, twirling her keys again. "You know I said that Maggie was too close to this case, but I've also wondered whether you're too close to it as well. You and Maggie? I haven't wanted to delve too much into your personal business, but it's clear that your 'past relationship'—" Tess drew air quotes around the last two words "—isn't so much in the past. Are you sure you can handle this case?"

His and Maggie's past relationship wasn't at all in the past anymore. And he planned to make sure a relationship with Maggie was his future, but he didn't tell Tess that. Not yet at least. He and Maggie still hadn't had a heart-to-heart, and despite the mind-blowing sex they'd shared, he didn't know what she was thinking. Heck, if he was being truthful with himself, he was afraid to find out exactly what she wanted. He could only hope she was feeling at least some of what he was feeling.

He realized he'd been silent for a beat too long. "I can handle it."

Tess cocked her head to the side and gave him a slight nod before rising. "Okay, then. Let me know if you need anything."

She turned back to him at the door. "Finding the ruby is why we were retained by the insurance company, and I don't think Maggie had anything to do with the theft. But we don't have unlimited time. If we don't find the ruby soon, the insurance agency will pull us and hire another firm."

He understood what she was saying. They'd lose access to the files and likely the people who could help clear Maggie's name. And another firm might think Maggie wasn't innocent.

"You need to find answers," Tess added. "Fast."

Chapter Twenty-One

"I can't imagine dealing with everything you've gone through in the last several days," Lisa said on the other end of the phone. "What can I do to help? Do you want me to come back down there?"

Maggie had just spent the last hour catching her best friend up on the events of the past several days and venting on the phone.

"No. I don't want to put you out." Lisa just having made the offer to drop everything and come stand by her side was enough to remind Maggie why she loved her friend. "I just needed someone to talk to."

"And I'm always here for that or whatever you need. You know that, right?"

"I do."

A beat of silence passed over the line.

"I feel like there's something else you want to say but aren't." Lisa always was perceptive.

"I slept with Kevin."

Lisa snorted. "That's not a surprise. I saw the way you two looked at each other."

"Yeah, it's not that simple." Maggie took a deep breath and told Lisa about her past relationship with Kevin while they were undergraduates and her miscarriage after they'd broken up.

"Maggie, I'm so sorry."

"I never expected to see Kevin again, but now that I have, I can't deny that there is still something there between us. But even if there is, does that mean it's healthy? Shouldn't I be looking forward, not backward?"

Lisa's sigh sounded through the line. "You know I don't believe in regrets or looking backward, but is that what this really is? I mean, you just said that there is something there between you two. Something in the here and now. I wouldn't necessarily say that it's unhealthy to explore what that might be."

"When has reuniting with an ex-boyfriend ever worked out in the end?"

"Frida Kahlo and Diego Rivera married, divorced and remarried, staying together until she passed away."

Maggie chuckled. "Of course you know that."

"What can I say? I know my art history."

Maggie couldn't help but be buoyed by Lisa's teasing.

"But really," Lisa said, becoming more serious. "I think you should think about what you really want. Forget the past. Think about the now and your future. And give yourself permission to forgive Kevin for walking away all those years ago. I'd hate for you to miss out on a good thing today because of choices you and Kevin made when you were just kids."

Maggie's phone beeped that she had a call coming in. She checked the screen and saw her father's photo.

"Lisa, I have to go. My dad is calling. But I heard you. I'll think about what you said."

"Good. Love ya."

"Love you too."

She ended the call with Lisa and clicked over to her father. She knew instantly that something was wrong.

"Dad?"

"Maggie?" Her father's words came out groggy.

"It's me, Dad."

"Maggie?"

"Dad? Are you okay?"

The silence on the other end of the phone spiked her anxiety.

"My head…my head hurts."

"Is Julie there, Dad?"

"Julie?"

Concern prickled at the back of her neck. Something was clearly wrong with her father.

She shoved her feet into her sneakers and grabbed her purse. "Did you fall? Dad, where are you?"

"Maggie, can you come over? My head hurts."

"I'm on my way, Dad. I'll be there in ten minutes. Stay on the phone with me, okay?" She was already moving to the front door.

"I think I need to lie down."

"Dad? Dad!"

The line went dead.

She dialed Kevin's number. The call went straight to voicemail.

"Kevin, something is wrong with my dad. I'm headed to his house now."

The drive from Kevin's house to her father's was fifteen minutes, but she made it in ten.

Her father's car wasn't in the driveway. She let herself into the house with her key.

"Dad? Julie? Anybody home?"

The house was quiet. Her heart galloped.

"Dad?"

A soft groan came from the back of the house.

"Dad?" She dropped her purse by the sofa in the living room as she hurried toward the back bedrooms.

Her father was on the floor of the main bedroom, next to the bed. She knelt next to him. "Oh my God, Dad. Here, let me help you up."

Her father gripped her arm tightly. "Hit me." His words slurred.

"Hit you? Did someone hit you, Dad?" Anger swelled in her chest. "Did Julie hit you?"

Her father shook his head. "Not…Julie. He hit me. From behind."

It was a struggle to get her father to his feet, but with his help she was finally able to get him onto the bed.

He rubbed the back of his head.

She put her hand to his head and felt a bump.

"He who, Dad?" she asked, panting slightly from a mix of exertion and rage. "Who hit you?"

"Ellison."

Her body went cold. "That's not possible. Ellison is dead."

Her father shook his head, but whether he was just trying to clear it, or he was disputing her claim about Ellison, she couldn't tell.

A thump came from the front of the house.

Her pulse quickened. Her father might have been confused about who hit him, but someone had. Someone who was still in the house.

She glanced around the room for a weapon but found nothing. Her purse was in the living room where she'd left it after she'd entered the house.

"Dad." She lowered her voice to a whisper. "Where is your phone?"

Her eyes darted around the room. Her father had called

her using his cell phone, but it was nowhere to be seen now. It didn't look like there was a landline in the house. At least, not in the bedroom.

The bedroom window was big enough for her to shimmy through. She could get out, run to a neighbor's house and call the police. But she couldn't leave her father.

She had to get to her purse and her cell phone.

"Stay here, Dad. I'm going to get my phone."

Her father gave a slight nod and squeezed her hand. She could tell he was in a lot of pain. Probably had a concussion. She needed to get him help quickly.

She forced herself to walk to the bedroom door and stuck her head out carefully, peering into the hallway.

It was empty.

She slid into the hall, closing the bedroom door after her. The hallway carpeting was the stiff, scratchy kind. It seemed to snap and crackle with each footstep.

There was a second bedroom across the hall from her father's room that was full of moving boxes.

Forcing herself to step as quietly as possible, she made her way down the hall toward the living room. Her father's house wasn't large. The living room could be seen from the kitchen and dining area. If the intruder was in any of those rooms, he'd see her as soon as she stepped out of the hall.

She stopped at the point where the hall opened onto the living room. Her heart hammered. She couldn't hear anything other than the sound of her own breathing, and that sounded like thunder rumbling through the entire house.

The living room looked to be empty.

She darted across the open space and grabbed her purse. She always kept her phone in the front pocket, but when she plunged her hand inside she felt nothing.

"Looking for this?"

Terror was a strange thing. Rationally, she knew she was more scared than she'd ever been in her life. Yet, at the sound of the voice that was almost as familiar to her as her own, a certain calmness washed over her.

She turned and, for the first time in three years, faced her ex-husband.

"Ellison."

Ellison stood in the passageway between the living room and the kitchen, a misshapen smile on his face. In one hand, he held her phone, and in the other, a knife.

"Ellison." Although her eyes were telling her that he was there, alive, her brain was struggling to catch up with the sight.

She was looking at a dead man. A very alive, dead man.

He looked different. His blond hair was now dark, almost black. The piercing blue eyes were now covered by brown contacts. He'd aged far more than the three it had been since she'd seen him. His skin darkened by a tan, but leathery looking. It looked like he'd been living hard, but being on the run would do that, she supposed.

"Ellison." She said his name again in an effort to make it all make sense in her head. "What…what are you doing here? How are you here?"

"I'm here for you," Ellison said, the words sending a sliver of fear through her. "You and the ruby."

"You…you stole the ruby?"

Ellison let out a laugh that sent a shiver down her spine. "You can get away with so much when you are dead."

She swallowed hard, already knowing the answer to the question she was about to ask. "And Kim?"

"I needed her help to steal the ruby. Wasn't hard to

convince her. But I couldn't take the chance that she'd turn on me later."

"You killed her?"

He shrugged, but it was more than enough of an answer. He'd killed her friend. And he planned to do the same to her.

She could make a run for the front door, but that would mean leaving her father, and she wouldn't do that. Even if she tried, she had no doubt that Ellison would catch her before she could get the door open. And he had a knife.

She looked into Ellison's eyes and saw a stranger. And hate. The man standing in front of her hated her. But why? She had to try to reach the man she'd married. He was still in there somewhere. At least, she hoped he was.

"Ellison, my father needs help. Let me call an ambulance for him."

"You want to help him? Where were you when I needed help?"

"I tried to be there for you."

"You tried? I lost my job. My reputation. My so-called friends. My home. You," he spat.

"We were divorced before the scandal."

"I never wanted that. I did everything for you. The money? That was all for you."

Maggie jerked with the realization of what he was saying. "I never asked you to steal for me. I wouldn't have."

"You didn't have to ask," he roared. "That's how much I loved you. And when I needed you, you deserted me."

"I tried to be there for you. I called. I reached out. But the pressure. The police suspected I'd helped you steal that money. The police and the press hounded me. I had to move to the West Coast to get away from it. Even after you died."

Ellison smirked. "Looks like that wasn't far enough." He tapped the knife against his thigh twice then flipped it, blade out.

"You don't have to do this. You have the money and now the ruby. Just take them and go."

"The money is gone. It takes a lot of money to live on the run. Why do you think I came for the ruby? And as for this?" He waved the knife at her. "I've had a lot of time to think about your betrayal. You have to pay."

She wasn't going to be able to reach him. If she wanted to get herself and her father out of this alive, she was going to have to fight.

She leaped toward the door, then as Ellison lurched after her, she spun, lashing out with a kick to his side. He hopped and stumbled backward, cursing. She pushed past him into the kitchen. There was another door there and, more importantly, a host of possible weapons she could use to defend herself.

She got lucky. Her father hadn't gotten around to cleaning up after lunch. The sink was full of dishes, including a large butcher knife. She grabbed it and turned just as Ellison stumbled into the kitchen.

"You're going to pay for that," he snarled, starting toward her.

Keys jangled in the front door.

Ellison froze.

"Boyd? Baby, are you okay?"

Maggie screamed, "Julie, run!"

She lunged at Ellison again, swiping out with the knife.

He jumped back, untouched. But the introduction of another person changed his odds. He swore then ran for the back door, shooting a venomous look over his shoulder at her before disappearing out of it.

"Maggie? What's going on? Are you okay? Where is Boyd?" Julie's eyes darted back and forth between the open back door and Maggie.

Maggie slid down onto the kitchen floor, her back against the lower cabinets.

Fire burned up her right arm. She looked down, catching sight of the bloody gash slashed there. He'd stabbed her.

She felt like she was going to throw up. Blood trickled from the wound on her arm and her head spun. "Dad, he needs help. Call 911," she stammered.

Then she passed out.

Chapter Twenty-Two

Maggie had regained consciousness by the time the EMTs arrived, her pride only a little worse for wear for having passed out at the sight of her own blood. She rode to the hospital in the ambulance with her father, Julie driving her car close behind. She'd called Kevin while the EMTs loaded her father into the ambulance and given him a quick summary of Ellison's attack on her father. Kevin was already there when the ambulance pulled up in the emergency room drive, standing next to his sister, Tanya.

She was relieved her father had a doctor that she knew cared. Tanya took charge immediately, barking out orders to the nurse and EMTs helping to move her father into the hospital. Kevin was by her side the moment she stepped out of the ambulance.

"I think my heart stopped when I got your message," Kevin said as they followed the gurney into the hospital. "Are you okay?"

"It's just a scratch." She held up her arm so he could see. The white bandage the EMT had applied in the ambulance was much bigger than was necessary. "I gave everyone a scare by passing out though."

A smile cracked through his worried expression. "Still can't stand to see your own blood."

"I'm not sure how anyone can."

She filled him in on her father's call and Ellison attacking her when she arrived at her father's house.

The shock she felt at seeing Ellison was mirrored on Kevin's face. "Ellison? How?"

"Apparently, he faked his death to get out of the embezzlement charge. I don't know how he did it, but, Kevin, I'm telling you he's alive." A tiny shiver shook through her.

"I'm not doubting you."

The doors to the waiting room opened, and Julie rushed through before he could say anything else. Julie scanned the visitors in the waiting room until her eyes landed on Maggie and Kevin in the far corner.

She rushed forward. "Has the doctor seen Boyd yet? Have they told you anything about his condition?"

Almost as if Julie had conjured her, Tanya stepped through the glass doors separating the emergency room from the waiting room.

"Maggie." Tanya stopped in front of the trio. "It's good to see you, although I wish it was under different circumstances."

"It's good to see you again too. I'm sorry to be so abrupt, but how is my father?"

"Nothing to be sorry for. Your father suffered a pretty serious concussion, but otherwise looks to be in good health. Because of his age, I want to keep him overnight just to keep an eye on him."

Maggie let go of the breath she felt like she'd been holding since she'd walked into her father's house and found him on the floor.

Julie squeezed her hand, tears of relief streaming down her face. "Can we see him?"

"You can see him now but only two at a time, and I'd

suggest you keep the visit brief. He needs to rest, but I anticipate releasing him tomorrow."

Julie and Maggie thanked the doctor.

"You two go," Kevin said. "I'll wait here."

Maggie froze when she saw her father in bed. His eyes were closed, and he looked so small and frail. His face was gray and ashen. His mortality slapped her in the face. Ellison's attack could have ended so much more tragically, and no matter what, one day her father wouldn't be here.

Julie squeezed her arm and gently pulled her forward toward her father's bed. "It's okay. He's okay," she whispered, seemingly reading the angst on Maggie's face.

"Dad," Maggie whispered.

Her father's eyes opened. It took several seconds for him to focus, but when he did, a small smile crossed his lips.

Julie slipped to the other side of the bed. Each woman took one of his hands.

"Did somebody die?" he quipped, looking from Maggie to Julie and back.

"I'm so sorry, Dad." Tears pooled in Maggie's eyes.

Her father pulled his hand from hers and cupped her face. "Hey, hey. You have nothing to be sorry for. This is not your fault."

"But Ellison…he was using you to get to me. He…"

Her father's face darkened. "He's out of his mind, but that's not your fault. I don't want you to blame yourself."

Her father's eyelids dropped.

Maggie shot a glance at Julie, who gave a slight shake of her head.

"Dad, I'm going to go and let you get some rest."

Her father's eyes opened again. His hand slid down to the bed and grasped hers. "Be careful. Stay safe."

She returned her father's squeeze. "I will. I promise. You get some rest." Maggie's gaze shifted to Julie. "You're going to stay with him?"

Julie smiled, looking down at Boyd with so much tenderness and devotion that it made Maggie's heart clench. "You just let them try to put me out of here."

Maggie was pretty sure that nothing less than a small army would be capable of dislodging Julie from her father's side. Still, the hospital wasn't a bunker. If Ellison wanted to get in, there were dozens of opportunities.

"I'll be back to check on you later."

"No need. I'm just going to be sleeping anyway. You just stay safe."

She leaned forward and pressed a kiss to her father's cheek. "I love you, Dad."

"I love you too, honey."

Kevin was on the phone when she returned to the waiting room. He hung up as she sailed through the doors.

"How is your father?"

She opened her mouth to answer, but all that came out was a choked sob.

Kevin pulled her into his arms and let her cry for several minutes. Once the deluge of tears slowed, she pulled back.

"Feel any better?" He grabbed a tissue from the box someone had left on the waiting room's coffee table.

Maggie dabbed her eyes and blew her nose. "A little. It was just…seeing my father so helpless."

"It can be hard to see our parents in a vulnerable state, but he's going to be okay according to the doctors, right?"

She nodded. "Right. Julie is staying in his room with him, but I'm scared that—"

"Ellison might try to hurt your father again as a way

to get to you. I thought of that too. Tess called Detective Francois, and she is sending one of our guys from West Investigations to guard your father until Ellison is in custody."

A boulder of stress rose from her shoulders. "Thank you." Ellison's screed at her father's house came back to her. "Ellison killed Kim," she said, a sob catching in her throat. "He admitted it to me."

From the look on his face, it appeared Kevin had already figured that out. He set his notebook aside and pulled her into another hug. "I know, sweetheart. I'm sorry."

"It's my fault. Ellison, he blames me. For the divorce. For pulling away during his embezzlement scandal."

Kevin lightly gripped her shoulders. "Hey, don't do that to yourself. You aren't to blame for any of this. He is. No one made him steal that money. Or the Viperé ruby. He took Kim's life. That's on him and only on him, understand?"

Her head understood, but her heart felt as if she should have known. The heavy weight of guilt wouldn't be lifting soon.

The doors to the waiting room opened again, and Detective Francois and Tess strode in.

"Ms. Scott, I'm happy to see you are relatively unharmed," the detective said. "Wishing your father a speedy recovery."

"Thank you, Detective," Maggie replied.

"Heard you kicked butt." Tess offered a tight smile. "Good girl."

Maggie sighed. "I don't know about that, but thanks."

"I know this is a trying time, but are you up for some

questions?" Detective Francois asked, taking out his phone.

Maggie sighed. More questions were the exact opposite of what she wanted to do at the moment, but she knew the detective was just doing his job. "Whatever I can do to help."

She went through the details, reiterating everything she'd told Kevin only minutes earlier. Francois's questions were nearly identical to Kevin's, but worded differently enough that a few smaller details she hadn't recalled before came back to her.

Detective Francois finally put his phone away. "Well, we have one major problem here."

Kevin's and Tess's slight nods showed they'd picked up on whatever the major problem was, but Maggie found herself left in the dark alone.

"Anyone care to fill me in on the problem?" Maggie asked.

"Ellison has been living off the grid and hiding his tracks for a long time," Tess started.

"He's practiced at being invisible. That's going to make it harder for us to find him," Kevin finished.

"I had patrols out driving a ten-mile radius within minutes of the 911 call, but he got past us somehow," Francois said, the frustration in his voice evident.

"Like I said, he's had a lot of time to practice being invisible. And since we can be sure he isn't using his real name, but we have no idea what name he is using, we don't really have a place to start looking," Kevin said.

"He's planned this for a long time." Tess frowned. "Harbored anger toward Maggie. He's not going to stop until he gets her."

"Tess," Kevin hissed.

Maggie pushed back the fear bubbling in her gut. "No, Tess is right. There's no point in sugarcoating it. Ellison is obsessed. He took the ruby because he needed the money, but he's stayed because he wants me. Dead."

Their quartet was silent for a long moment.

"We need to draw him out on our terms," Tess finally said.

"No," Kevin barked.

"The brass would never sign off on something like that," Detective Francois said, shaking his head.

"So it doesn't have to be an LAPD operation," Tess shot back.

"I said no." Kevin's bark had turned into a growl.

"Excuse me." Maggie raised her hand as if she were a pupil in school. "Again, could someone tell me what it is we are talking about here?"

Tess looked at her. "Bait. Specifically, using you as bait to draw out Ellison."

"How many times do I have to say it—"

Tess held up a hand. "You didn't have to say it the first time. I know you're against it, but if we weren't talking about Maggie, would you be as opposed to the idea?"

"It's too dangerous," Kevin said.

"Not an answer," Tess shot back. "Maggie is already in danger, and we don't know when Ellison is going to pop up again. He's waited years to come out of the shadows. He could very well go back into hiding, wait until our guard is down and pop up again. We have an opportunity now, and we should press it."

"She's right," Maggie interjected.

"She is not right."

"Look, I don't like it either, but she's right about Ellison going back underground. I don't want to live my life looking over my shoulder. If we have the chance to grab him now, I say we take it. All the better if we can get the Viperé ruby back at the same time and save West Investigations' reputation."

"I don't give a damn about West Investigations' reputation," Kevin growled.

"Not the best way to get on your new boss's good side," Tess chided.

"He doesn't mean that," Maggie said, shooting Kevin a look.

"If I thought he did, I'd fire him," Tess responded.

Detective Francois took a step away from the group. "I need to get back out there and try to catch Ellison Coelho using less...radical means. LAPD can't be involved in dangling Ms. Scott as bait, but if I can be of any help, you have my number."

Maggie guessed that meant he didn't suspect her in the crimes any longer. That was some relief. "Thank you, Detective."

Detective Francois gave her a brisk nod then strode from the waiting room.

"This is a terrible idea," Kevin said.

"If you have a better one, I'm all ears," Tess shot back. His frown said it all.

"I'm in," Maggie said. She reached for Kevin's hand and looked him in the eye. "I'm in. I trust you and Tess, and I want to end this now."

Kevin gripped both her hands and leaned down until his forehead rested against hers. He closed his eyes. Out of the side of her eye, Maggie saw Tess slide away.

"I don't want to lose you," he whispered.

"I don't want to lose you either. This is the best shot that we have right now."

They stood for a moment more before Kevin pulled back. His gaze tracked to Tess standing a polite distance away now. "What do you have in mind?"

Chapter Twenty-Three

Kevin sat in his office, frustrated. Detective Francois hadn't been willing to dangle Maggie as bait, but the police department was willing to bend the truth a bit to get the public off their backs. Francois put out a press statement saying the department believed they knew who the suspect was in the theft of the Viperé ruby and Kim Sumika's murder. The statement made it clear that the crimes had been targeted and that the police believed the culprit had likely fled the country.

And in the week since Ellison had attacked Boyd Scott, Kevin could almost convince himself that the police's statement was correct and that Ellison had done the rational thing and run. Neither West Investigations nor the LAPD had been able to find a single trace of Ellison.

But Kevin's gut told him that after everything he'd done, Ellison wasn't going to give up on getting to Maggie.

Despite his attempts to convince her not to, Maggie had moved back into her cottage. West Investigations had set up discreet surveillance on her at home and at work. Since Detective Francois had made it clear Maggie was no longer a suspect, Maggie was pushing to get her job back. Gustev and Tutwilder were both dragging their feet and resisting though. Neither were happy to have her back at the museum, but Maggie was determined to fight for her job. She wasn't going to allow Ellison's actions to ruin the life she'd built for a second time. Kevin admired her for that gumption.

There was a knock on the door to his office. Tess stood there, practically vibrating. "Hey, we have a lead on the ruby."

His pulse quickened. A lead on the ruby meant a lead on Ellison's whereabouts. "What's the lead?"

"A source tipped me to an underground auction for black-market art. My source says the guy running it was bragging about some, and I quote, 'big, honking gem that's going to bring in a boatload of money.'"

Kevin grinned. "LAPD?"

"I've already called Detective Francois, and he spoke to my source and found him credible. The cops are working on search warrants right now." Tess's smile grew wider. "And since I've been such a Good Samaritan, Detective Francois has allowed us to tag along."

Kevin rose, moving around his desk before she'd finished the sentence. "Let's go."

POLICE VEHICLES CROWDED the parking lot of the elementary school a half block away from the target house. They were lucky that the estate homes sat several yards back from the street. Kevin and Tess joined the half a dozen uniformed officers standing at the trunk of one of the patrol cars listening to Detective Francois give instructions.

"Okay," Francois said, fastening the strap on the bulletproof vest he wore. "Our source says that there is a high-value auction of various stolen goods going on inside the property three homes down from here. The real estate records show it's owned by a foreign national from Sweden who is supposedly out of the country. We are going to breach quickly and detain everyone inside. We want to take everyone in safely and make sure we don't damage any priceless art or jewels or whatever else they are selling in there." Detective Francois gestured toward where Kevin and Tess stood at the back of the pack. "These two are headed in with us. They are on the trail of the Viperé ruby."

A ripple fluttered through the group as heads turned to check them out.

"We're going in as four teams of four. Two through the front and two around the back." Francois checked the magazine on his gun then looked up at the group. "Everybody ready?"

Kevin adjusted the bulletproof vest he wore and checked his own gun.

There was a ripple of agreement before everyone peeled off into groups of four. One of the officers carried a ram. The teams advance toward the house, quickly and quietly, the first two teams peeling off and heading around the house toward the back. The front rooms of the house were empty, the lack of lights making it appear empty, but the house was large, easily six to seven thousand square feet, with two aboveground levels.

Kevin and Tess's team brought up the rear heading to the front of the house. The two teams stopped on either side of the front door waiting for the breach signal. It was late, and the neighborhood was quiet. Cool air brushed over his skin, but adrenaline and anxiousness had beads of sweat forming on his temple despite the breeze.

"Team three and four in position," the radio on one of the uniformed officer's shoulder crackled.

Detective Francois held up three fingers. The first finger dropped soundlessly. Then the second. With the last finger, Francois barked, "Go! Go! Go!"

The officer with the ram advanced, swinging it at the door at full speed. The door cracked under the force and swung open. The rest of the team wasted no time flooding through the open door, yelling out commands for the inhabitants of the house to "freeze" and "put their hands up." The other two teams flooded in from the back of the house.

The teams that had come through the back door moved forward, clearing the rooms on the main floor quickly. But it was clear from the angry shrieks and screams that came from the basement that was where the action was.

Kevin followed Tess, their team leader, and one of the other teams down the basement stairs. The basement was finished with marble floors, two chandeliers and a full bar running along one of the rear walls.

A small stage had been set up at the other end of the basement. People, most clad in business attire, were scattered in the rows of chairs facing the stage. Three paintings, abstracts that looked like nothing more than paint splatters, rested on easels in a semicircle on the stage. A gold statue of a dragon held a prominent place on a podium in front of the paintings. Anyone could be forgiven for thinking they'd walked into an auction house or gallery instead of the basement of a multimillion dollar home in the suburbs of Los Angeles.

"Nobody moves!" Francois called out. "Keep your hands where we can see them."

Two of the men in the crowd stood, but the third team of uniformed officers hustling down the staircase quickly snuffed out any errant thoughts of fleeing.

Kevin scanned the faces of the men in the crowd looking for Ellison, but Maggie's ex wasn't there.

"Lombard. Stenning. Over here. I think there's something you'd like to see," Detective Francois called.

He followed Tess. Detective Francois held back a curtain separating the front of the stage. Several more items waited behind the curtain for their turn on the stage. Kevin's eyes were drawn to one. One sparkling, large, red jewel. The Viperé ruby, nestled in a black velvet cushion in a locked glass case.

Tess turned to him with a grin. "Bingo!"

It wouldn't be official until the insurance company's gemologist evaluated and signed off on it, but it looked like they'd just found the Viperé ruby.

MAGGIE WAS FRUSTRATED. Without a job, she was listless and unsure what to do with her days. She couldn't spend every minute with Kevin, and wouldn't want to if she could. He had a job, and even though he was spending the majority of his time searching for Ellison, he had other cases he had to oversee for West Investigations.

Her father had been released from the hospital, and at her urging, he and Julie had gone to Julie's son's house in Arizona. Kevin assured her that he had a man he could trust watching over the family, although Maggie had chosen to keep that piece of information from her father. She didn't want to worry him more than necessary, but she was relieved that her father and Julie were safe. Both of them assured her that they didn't blame her for Ellison's attack, but Maggie couldn't shake the guilt. She'd brought Ellison into their lives in the first place, and it was her Ellison was really after.

Since moving back into her cottage, she was under

constant surveillance by the West team, but so far Ellison hadn't taken the bait. With time on her hands, she spent it researching and racking her brain for where Ellison could be hiding out. In this day and age, it was nearly impossible for a person to go completely off the grid. They just had to figure out where Ellison would go. She knew him best, and she was their best chance of doing that.

The doorbell rang, and then someone pounded on the door. "Ms. Scott? It's Detective Decker."

"Yes."

"Ma'am, I received a call from Detective Francois. He believes Ellison Coelho is in the area. He'd like me to stick close to you until he gets here. Do you mind if I come in?"

Her pulse rate picked up its pace. Ellison was close. That meant they had a chance to catch him and end this nightmare tonight.

She looked out the peephole. The detective stood too close for her to see his face, but he held his badge up so she could see it.

She unlocked the dead bolt. As she opened the door, a hard push came from the other side, wrenching the doorknob from her hands and sending the door crashing open.

Ellison stood on the other side of the door, a gun in his hand. "Surprise."

She turned to run but didn't get far.

Excruciating pain vaulted through the back of her head. Then everything went black.

When she awoke, Maggie's head hurt worse than it ever had before. Her hands and feet were tied, and there was a piece of masking tape over her mouth. She was on her side, bouncing against a hard surface. In a car. The trunk of a car, to be specific.

Ellison had her. He intended to kill her.

And Kevin had no idea where she was.

Panic started to rise in her chest. She pushed it back down. She needed to keep her head if she had any hope of getting out of this alive. She needed a plan. It was dark in the trunk, but Ellison had tied her hands together in front of her.

She groped around the floor of the trunk hoping to find something, anything, to defend herself with. But there was nothing.

The car stopped abruptly, slamming her into the back of the trunk then rolling her forward.

She heard the car's door open then slam closed. Gravel crunched.

Ellison was coming.

The trunk popped open, and she blinked rapidly. Her eyes adjusted to the moonlight filtering in the open trunk, and she looked up into the mottled face of the man she'd once thought she'd loved.

"I'm going to get you out of the trunk. If you try anything, I will shoot you." He held up the gun to underscore his point. "Do you understand?"

She nodded.

Ellison grabbed her tied hands and yanked her up. He lifted her out of the trunk then roughly dropped her to the ground next to the back tires of the car.

She took the opportunity to scan the area. They were on a dock. Next to a warehouse that looked to be closed.

He slammed the trunk then reached for her again.

He pulled her to her feet, pushing her toward the warehouse.

Chapter Twenty-Four

He had her.

Kevin tried to control his panic, but it was a losing battle. It was all he could think about. Ellison had Maggie and was doing God only knew what to her. She might not even still be alive.

He pulled to a stop on Maggie's street, which was full of vehicles—squad cars, marked police sedans, black West Investigations SUVs and an ambulance.

Please, God, don't let that be for Maggie.

He got out of the car and ran toward Detective Francois.

"Maggie, is she—?" He couldn't bring himself to say the words.

The tech who'd been monitoring the security system at Maggie's house had called as soon as he'd realized the man at Maggie's door wasn't a police officer. He'd said that Ellison had knocked Maggie out and carried her out of the range of the camera, but what if he'd been wrong. What if Ellison had just taken her out of the range of the camera to—

"The ambulance isn't for Maggie," Tess said, stepping in front of him and stopping him from racing for the ambulance.

Francois radiated anger. "It's for the man I had on her

house tonight. Detective Decker. He took one gunshot to the torso through the car window. The EMTs are preparing to take him to the hospital now."

As if they'd heard Francois's words, the ambulance's sirens whooped, and the vehicle lurched forward and down the street, increasing in speed as it went.

Kevin worked to slow his racing heart. It wasn't Maggie in the back of the ambulance on the way to the hospital. That was good. "What do we know?"

"Our cameras caught Ellison walking up to Maggie's door at 9:25 p.m.," Tess started in a calm, focused voice. "Kept his head down, but he had Decker's badge around his neck and a holstered sidearm, so our tech thought it was Decker at first. Maggie must have thought so too. She opened the door to him after he held his badge up to the peephole. It wasn't until he pushed open the door and clocked Maggie over the head with the gun that the tech realized something was wrong."

Kevin tamped down the anger that swelled in him at hearing that Ellison had hurt Maggie. He needed to remain professional, clearheaded, if he was going to find her in time.

"The tech tried to reach Decker, but he didn't answer."

The ambulance was gone now, but they all instinctively turned to look at the unmarked sedan with the missing driver-side window that CSI was now crawling over.

Tess cleared her throat. "When he couldn't reach Decker, he called Francois."

"I had a squad car dispatched immediately. The unit found Decker when they arrived, one uniform started CPR while the other went into Ms. Scott's house."

"Ellison and Maggie were gone by then." Tess picked

up the story again. "He parked out of view of the cameras, so we don't have a tag, make or model."

"That suggests that Ellison knew where the cameras were. And if he was able to sneak up on a trained detective—"

"He's probably been casing the house and neighborhood," Tess finished his thought.

"How is that possible?" Kevin wanted to scream. The LAPD and West Investigations, one of the best security firms in the nation, were supposed to have been protecting Maggie, and they both failed?

Tess frowned. "There are always blind spots. You know that. We're doing the best we can, but Ellison has had years of practice being invisible. Hiding himself from people he didn't want to see him."

"I have officers canvassing the area for possible witnesses," Francois spoke up. "It's possible someone saw something or someone's security system caught the car."

"And if no one did?" Kevin asked although the answer was obvious. If they didn't get a break, they were screwed.

"Detective Francois, sir," a uniformed officer called. Francois ambled away.

"Kevin, I think you should head back to West headquarters," Tess said.

"The hell I will."

"You are too close to this. You've been too close to this case. I should have taken you off days ago. And now..." She shook her head. "I can't use you if your personal feelings for Maggie are going to cloud your professional judgment."

He glared at Tess. "I'm not going anywhere."

Tess glared right back. "I can make it an order—"

"Lombard. Stenning." Francois waved them over. "I think we got something here."

Kevin whirled away from his boss, stalking over to where Francois stood with the uniform. He hadn't noticed him earlier, but a teenaged boy stood with the two men. Long wisps of curly red hair fell in the boy's face, and he fidgeted from one foot to the other.

"This is Allan. Son, can you repeat what you just told me?"

The teen let out a heavy sigh. "Again?"

"One more time," Francois encouraged him.

"Okay, I mean, like, I was out, okay, I snuck out to see my girl, and I'm just walking, right?" He looked at the adults around him as if walking might not be familiar to the old folks.

"Got it, kid. You were walking," Kevin said, hoping to urge the story on faster.

"So yeah, I'm walking. My girl lives a couple blocks down that way." He pointed south of where they stood. "Then all of a sudden, I hear this lady scream, and then I see a man carrying a woman, like, fireman style over his shoulder and whatnot. And I'm like, whoa, that's probably not cool."

Kevin was finding it hard not to shake the story out of the kid to get him to talk faster. Tess must have sensed his agitation.

She gave a slight shake of her head.

"So then I was like, I can't let him see me, you know. So I ducked down behind that car there." The boy turned and pointed at a black Range Rover. "But like I said, something didn't seem right, so I snapped a picture of the car."

"You have a photo of the car the man put the woman in?" Francois said, testily.

"Oh, yeah." The teen reached into his coat pocket and pulled out his phone. "I must have forgotten to tell you that part. I got a photo of the tag and everything. Wanna see?" He held the phone up to his face to unlock it.

Kevin didn't wait for the teen to find the photo. He snatched the phone from the boy's hand.

"Hey, man! That's mine."

Kevin ignored the teen, navigating to his photo gallery while Tess assured the boy that he'd get his phone back in a moment.

He found the photos quickly. A silver, four-door Toyota Corolla. A dime a dozen, but the teen had captured a clear picture of the license plate. He sent copies of the photographs to himself, Tess and Francois before handing the phone back to the boy.

"You did a good job," he said to the teen. "Stop sneaking out at night though. You're going to get yourself in trouble." Kevin turned and started after Tess, who, like Francois, was already on the phone probably having someone pull the registration for the license.

THE CAR BELONGED to Charles and Louise Bennett, a couple in their seventies. The computer guru at West Investigations tracked down an address and phone number for the couple, worried that they might have become Ellison's victims too. Luckily, they were out of town in their winter home in Florida. As far as they knew, the car was parked in the garage at their San Pedro home.

The Bennetts had given permission to search their property. They had a larger home on several acres that afforded them the privacy that was elusive in much of Los Angeles. Ellison had to have spent a significant amount of time formulating his plan. If they dug deep enough, they'd probably find some connection between him and the Ben-netts, even a tenuous one. How else would he know that they spent part of the year in Florida? He'd had years to come up with a nearly foolproof plan. Who knows how much time they had to find Maggie before it was too late for her? It might already be too late for all they knew.

Kevin, Tess, Detective Francois and several other of-ficers fanned out in the house. Despite the size of the home, it didn't take long to determine that Ellison and Maggie weren't there. It was equally clear, though, that someone had been living in the house while the Bennetts were away. Dishes cluttered the countertops. The bed in the main bedroom was unmade. Wet bath towels lay on the bathroom floor. A dark blue Tucson was parked in the garage, but the silver Toyota Corolla that should have been next to it was gone.

"Damnit! Where are they?" Kevin's chest felt as if it were caving in on itself. He'd never been more afraid.

Tess clasped a hand on his shoulder and squeezed. "Keep your head in the game. We'll find her."

He nodded, taking several deep breaths then joining the search of the house for clues to where Ellison may have taken Maggie.

He crossed the sunken living room to the home of-fice. One long wall was a floor-to-ceiling bookcase that matched the oversize walnut-colored desk that dominated the room. A sleek silver computer sat on the neat-as-a-pin desk.

Kevin sat in the leather executive chair and turned on the computer. The login and password were taped to the monitor. What better way for Ellison to stay off the grid than to use someone else's Wi-Fi and login information.

Kevin opened the browser and went to the history, frustrated to find that it had been deleted.

"Try the cache," Tess said, coming up behind him at the desk.

"The cache?"

"Move." She shooed him out of the chair, taking the seat for herself and clicking the mouse. "Everyone knows to clear their browser history if they don't want someone to come behind them and see what they've been searching. But most people don't think about the cache. That's where the computer stores certain data—images, fonts, that sort of thing—that make it easier for you to download the same pages again later. That can tell us a lot too."

Tess clicked the mouse a few more times, and a logo popped up on screen.

"MaxPrint," Kevin read the name off. "Never heard of it."

"Let's see." Tess opened a browser and put the name of the company along with "Los Angeles area" into the search box.

The search engine returned a webpage. Bright red letters at the top of the page screamed that, as of a few years ago, MaxPrint had closed its doors permanently. Tess copied the address for the company and pasted it into a map search box.

A map pinpointing the defunct business's location opened up in a new tab. She zoomed in on what looked like an industrial area of mostly businesses.

"That must be where he took her." Tess looked up at him from where she sat. "The building is probably still empty. Ellison would have made sure of that. And since it is late, he'd have all night before anyone from one of the surrounding businesses showed up."

"Francois!" Kevin yelled, already heading for the door.

The detective met him in the foyer of the house. He quickly explained what he and Tess had found and their theory.

"I'll get squad cars rolling that way now." Francois was already dialing a number on his phone.

"Tess and I are on our way," Kevin said.

Maggie was in that warehouse. He could feel it.

Hang on, baby. I'm coming.

THE CONCRETE FLOOR was cracked, little more than rubble in several places, and the air was sour and smelled of mold. The space was mostly empty, but there were signs of the business that used to inhabit the space. Broken wooden pallets, a metal desk and office chair. Wires hung precariously from the ceiling, and most of the windows that lined the top of the wall had been broken, jagged shards of glass protruding dangerously.

She heard a squeak as they entered, followed by the pitter-patter of paws that signaled she and Ellison were not the only two animals in the space.

But rats were the least of her problems.

Ellison led her to the chair and pushed her into it. "Don't move. I'm going to take the tape off of your mouth. If you try anything…" He held the gun up.

She yelped when he ripped the tape off.

"Why are you doing this?"

He glared at her. "I already told you why."

"Ellison, this…this has to stop. I'm sorry if I hurt you. But this, you aren't going to get away with it. The police know you're alive. They know you stole the money, the ruby, that you killed Kim and attacked my father." She said the last words with more than a little bitterness. She'd never forgive him for hurting her father.

He chortled. "Then what's one more notch on my record, huh? It was so much harder to live on the run than I expected. Five hundred thousand dollars doesn't go nearly as far as I'd have hoped. New identities. Constant moving. Staying off the radar. It's expensive." He propped himself against the side of the desk. "When I saw that the Larimer would be exhibiting the Viperé and that you were curating the exhibit, well, it had to be a sign."

"A sign?"

"Yes. The ruby is priceless. And if I could steal it and make it look like you'd done it then disappear, well, that had a certain symmetry to it, don't you see? Only you wouldn't just be pretending to be dead like I was."

"No one will believe I stole the ruby now, and if you kill me, Kevin will hunt you to the ends of the earth."

Ellison's laughter grew louder. He threw his arms out wide and tipped his head back. "Let him come." He looked her in the eyes. "I lost everything when you walked out on me. I have nothing left to lose."

They were the words of a man who was lost to madness. There was nothing behind Ellison's gaze. She knew he would kill her if she didn't do something.

She lunged up out of the chair at him, ready to fight for her life.

Luck was on her side. She caught Ellison off guard. By the time he thought to raise the gun, she was driving her shoulder into his stomach.

He yelped and staggered backward.

She'd never punched anyone in her life, didn't know the first thing about doing it properly, but she made a fist and swung for Ellison's face, catching him on the chin.

He had four inches and at least thirty pounds on her, but she knew that if she lost this fight, it would be her last. She used that knowledge, that fear, as fuel, punching and kicking like a wild animal.

Ellison put his hands up in self-defense, the hand with the gun coming around in a circular motion and catching her in the temple.

Now she staggered, falling down to her knees.

She looked up to find Ellison pointing the gun at her. His lips moved, but she couldn't hear him. It sounded like the world had exploded into screams.

All she could see was the gun pointed at her.

Then Ellison jerked backward, the gun flying out of his hand.

Thunder rolled over the warehouse, and it took a moment for her to realize that it wasn't thunder but a helicopter. The screams had come from the police officers that had stormed into the warehouse.

Then Kevin was there, on his knees beside her.

"Maggie, baby, are you okay? Talk to me."

She looked past Kevin to where Ellison lay on the floor. She couldn't see him because he was surrounded by half a dozen armed officers. "Is he dead?"

"Don't worry about him." Kevin slid one arm around her waist and another under her legs. "Let's get you out of here."

She rested her head on his shoulder and let him carry her to safety.

Chapter Twenty-Five

Maggie didn't complain when Kevin insisted she go to the hospital and get checked out this time. Ellison faking his death, stealing the Viperé ruby and attempting to kill her had made international news. She'd had to turn off her cell phone, and Detective Francois had stationed several officers at Kim's house, her house, to keep the vultures off the property.

Ellison was dead. The police were still searching the home he'd been hiding out in, but it appeared he'd documented his plan to steal the Viperé and his growing hatred for Maggie in a journal. From what the police had already been able to piece together, it appeared that Ellison had decided that the best way to avoid the consequences of his embezzlement back in New York was to fake his death. He'd done a sufficiently good job at hiding most of the money, so he had the means to live comfortably if he scaled back his lifestyle. Unfortunately, scaling back was the opposite of what he'd done. In less than three years, he'd blown through almost all of the half a million dollars he'd been able to squirrel away. With no money and nothing but time, his thoughts had turned to how to get his hands on more money.

The browser history on his computer showed that he'd

been keeping track of Maggie and her new job, his bitterness toward her perceived slight of him during the embezzlement investigation growing. When he saw the announcement for the upcoming Viperé ruby exhibit, a plan to steal it began to take shape in his head. Being dead allowed Ellison a lot of latitude for sneaking into Maggie's life. He discovered Kim's gambling habit and debts and, using a fake persona, convinced Kim to give him the security code for the museum's cameras as well as details about the donors' open house. Maggie wasn't initially a target. Ellison had no idea she would still be there on the night of the theft, but seeing her ignited all the animosity he'd built up toward her, and his rage had taken control. He'd decided that she had to pay for what he saw as abandoning him. He was the one who had broken into her house and attacked her father.

There was a knock on her hospital room door. She looked up to find Kevin standing in the doorway. He held a white paper bag in one hand and a coffee cup in the other.

Her stomach growled, and she realized that she was starving.

Kevin put the bag and coffee down on the bedside table then leaned over and kissed her lightly on the lips. "How are you feeling?"

"Like I'd like to get out of this hospital bed and into my own bed."

Kevin kissed her again. "Soon. Let the doctors run all their tests then I'll take you home."

She smiled up at the man she'd loved since she was twenty, the man she now knew she'd always love. "That sounds good." She wiggled her eyebrows.

He laughed. "I wasn't suggesting anything." He sobered a touch. "But I do think it might be a good idea if you stayed with me. Just for a few days. It's a bit of a madhouse at your place right now."

She sighed. "So I've heard. I talked to my father and Julie and let them know I was okay."

Kevin nodded. "I know. Tess agreed to keep a man from West on them for another day or two. Just to be on the safe side."

Maggie let out a breath of relief. "Thank you. I know Ellison is no longer a threat to me or my dad, but..."

"But you need time to process everything. I get it." Kevin reached for her hand. "Take your time. I'm not going anywhere."

She squeezed his hand, for the first time in days feeling light, despite being in a hospital bed. "That's a promise I'm going to hold you to."

Kevin leaned down, his lips grazing hers. "Hold me tight."

Epilogue

Maggie stood in the small party room with Julie and Julie's daughter, Sara. She felt butterflies soaring in her stomach. She could hear the sound of the harpist and the buzz of the wedding guests floating on the breeze being carried in from the garden. Everyone was waiting.

She looked in the mirror, touching her hair, which had been twisted into an elaborate updo with curls falling forward to frame her face.

"You look gorgeous," Julie said from the other side of the room.

Maggie turned and smiled at the bride. "We're supposed to be telling *you* that."

Julie really did make a beautiful bride. She wore a champagne-colored tea-length dress and red satin heels with a sparkly buckle. She'd spent the last three months all but glued to Maggie's father's side, nursing him back to health. Her father and Julie had decided that they didn't want to wait any longer than necessary to make their relationship official, although as far as Maggie was concerned, Julie was already officially part of their family. There was no need for a quick wedding, but since that was what her father and Julie wanted, Maggie made it her mission to make it happen. She'd thrown herself into wedding planning with gusto.

Kevin had gently suggested, more than once, that her enthusiasm for wedding planning might be an offshoot of the lingering guilt she felt over Ellison's attack on her father. It was true that she still struggled with guilt from having brought Ellison into their lives, but she was working through it. And she did want her father and Julie to have the wedding of their dreams. Even if they only had three months to make it happen.

Thankfully, Julie's daughter and sons had also been on board with making their mother's wedding everything she wanted. And Boyd and Julie wanted to keep the nuptials small and intimate. They'd divided up the to-do list, and together they'd been able to get the flowers, cake, food, venue, dresses, tuxedos and musicians on board in less than ninety days. And in the process, Maggie had begun building the first threads of a bond with her soon-to-be stepsister and stepbrothers.

"My hands are shaking," Julie said.

"Here, Mom," Sara said, thrusting a champagne flute in her mother's hand. "Drink this. It will calm your nerves."

Julie took a long sip and pressed her palm flat against her stomach. "Whew. I don't want to be tipsy going down the aisle."

Sara waved away her mother's concern with a laugh. "Don't worry. Rick can carry you down the aisle if he has to."

Maggie joined her soon-to-be stepsister and stepmother in laughter. At six three and built like a professional football player, Julie's oldest son, Rick, would have no problem carrying his mother down the aisle. But Julie dispelled that notion quickly.

"No way." Julie set the half-full champagne glass down

on a side table. "I want to get to the end of that aisle on my own steam and greet my groom."

Maggie's heart swelled with the love she saw in Julie's eyes. "Well, let's get this show on the road then."

The women shared a quick three-way hug before marching into the anteroom where Rick, Julie's younger son, Thomas, and one of Boyd's friends from the senior center waited to escort them down the aisle.

Maggie slipped her arm through Thomas's and grabbed her bouquet of pink and off-white roses. Together, the wedding party stepped forward as the harpist began playing the wedding march. They walked into the garden, which was full of colorful flowers, and faced the sparkling manmade lake that was the centerpiece of the resort's attractions. It was the perfect backdrop for Julie and her father to exchange their vows, but all Maggie could see was Kevin.

He looked more handsome than she'd ever seen him in a dark blue suit that looked as if each thread had been spooled just for him. His smile lit up his face, and his eyes never left hers as her father and Julie pledged their undying love to each other. Maggie was ridiculously happy. Not just for her father, but because she and Kevin had decided to give their relationship another shot. They'd both been through a lot and made mistakes when they were younger, but she knew that they were wiser and stronger as individuals now. They'd spent a lot of time talking, about what they'd done wrong and about what they wanted out of a relationship and life now. She felt in her heart that it would last this time. They'd agreed to take it slow, but she knew Kevin was the man she was supposed to spend her life with. He'd always been that man.

Later that night, with the reception in full swing, Kevin

swept Maggie outside onto the patio where her father and Julie had exchanged their vows just hours earlier. They walked hand in hand to the edge of the lake, a bottle of champagne in Maggie's hand and two champagne flutes in Kevin's.

She tapped her glass against Kevin's before taking a sip. "It was a beautiful wedding, wasn't it?"

"I don't know," Kevin answered. "All I could see was you."

She set her champagne glass on the patio and kissed him.

After a long moment, Kevin broke off the kiss. "I worried that it was too early, but I don't think I can wait any longer." He fell to one knee and slid a little black box from his trouser pocket. "I want to spend the rest of my life with you. Marry me?"

A single tear fell from Maggie's eye, but her heart swelled and the smile she wore lit up her insides. "Yes," she answered, gazing down at the man she loved.

Kevin slid a brilliant square-cut diamond onto her finger then stood, sweeping her into his arms. "Since you're now an expert in pulling together beautiful weddings quickly, how about we set the wedding day for three months from now?"

Maggie laughed, her insides flip-flopping at the thought of another wedding. "I'm not sure I can wait that long to be your wife."

Kevin's grin spread from ear to ear. "That's just what I hoped to hear."

* * * * *

*Look for the next book in K.D. Richards's miniseries
West Investigations when* The Perfect Murder
goes on sale in November!

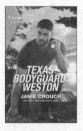